Miss Meredith

Contents

I

A Family of Four

It was about a week after Christmas, and we—my mother, my two sisters, and myself—were sitting, as usual, in the parlour of the little house at Islington. Tea was over, and Jenny had possession of the table, where she was engaged in making a watercolour sketch of still life by the light of the lamp, whose rays fell effectively on her bent head with its aureole of Titian-coloured hair—the delight of the Slade school—and on her round, earnest young face as she lifted it from time to time in contemplation of her subject.

My mother had drawn her chair close to the fire, for the night was very cold, and the fitful crimson beams played about her worn, serene, and gentle face, under its widow's cap, as she bent over the sewing in her hands.

A hard fight with fortune had been my mother's from the day when, a girl of eighteen, she had left a comfortable home to marry my father for love. Poverty and sickness—those two redoubtable dragons—had stood ever in the path. Now, even the love which had been by her side for so many years, and helped to comfort them, had vanished into the unknown. But I do not think she was unhappy. The crown of a woman's life was hers; her children rose up and called her blest.

At her feet sat my eldest sister, Rosalind, entirely absorbed in correcting a bundle of proof-sheets which had arrived that morning from *Temple Bar*. Rosalind was the genius of the family, a full-blown London B.A., who occasionally supplemented her earnings as coach and lecturer by writing for the magazines. She had been engaged, moreover, for the last year or two, to a clever young journalist, Hubert Andrews by name, and the lovers were beginning to look forward to a speedy termination to their period of waiting.

I, Elsie Meredith, who was neither literary nor artistic, neither picturesque like Jenny nor clever like Rosalind, whose middle place in the family had always struck me as a fit symbol of my own mediocrity—I, alone of all these busy people, was sitting idle. Lounging in the arm-chair which faced my mother's, I twisted and retwisted, rolled and unrolled, read and reread a letter which had arrived for me that morning, and whose contents I had been engaged in revolving in my mind throughout the day.

"Well, Elsie," said my mother at last, looking up with a smile from her work, "have you come to any decision, after all this hard thinking?"

"I suppose it will be 'Yes,'" I answered rather dolefully; "Mrs. Gray seems to think it a quite unusual opportunity." And I turned again to the letter, which contained an offer of an engagement for me as governess in the family of the Marchesa Brogi, at Pisa.

"I should certainly say 'Go,'" put in Rosalind, lifting her dark expressive face from her proofs; "if it were not for Hubert I should almost feel inclined to go myself. You will gain all sorts of experience, receive all sorts of new impressions. You are shockingly ill-paid at Miss Cumberland's, and these people offer a very fair salary. And if you don't like it, it is always open to you to come back."

"We should all miss you very much, Elsie," added my mother; "but if it is for your good, why, there is no more to be said."

"Oh, of course we should miss her horribly," cried Rosalind, in her impetuous fashion, gathering together the scattered proof-sheets as she spoke; "you mustn't think we want to get rid of you." And the little thoughtful pucker between her straight brows disappeared as she laid her hand with a smile on my knee. I pressed the inky, characteristic fingers in my own. I am neither literary nor artistic, as I said before, but I have a little talent for being fond of people.

"I'm sure I don't know what I shall do without you," put in Jenny, in her deliberate, serious way, making round, grey eyes at me across the lamplight. "It isn't that you are such a good critic, Elsie, but you have a sort of feeling for art which helps one more than you have any idea of."

I received very meekly this qualified compliment, without revealing the humiliating fact that my feeling for art had probably less to do with the matter than my sympathy with the artist; then observed, "It seems much waste, for me, of all of us, to be the first to go to Italy."

"I would rather go to Paris," said Jenny, who belonged, at this stage of her career, to a very advanced school of æsthetics, and looked upon Raphael as rather out of date. "If only someone would buy my picture I would have a year at Julian's; it would be the making of me."

"For heaven's sake, Jenny, don't take yourself so seriously," cried Rosalind, rising and laying down her proofs; "one day, perhaps, I shall come across an art-student with a sense of humour—growing side by side with a blue rose. Now, Elsie," she went on, turning to me as Jenny, with a reproachful air of superior virtue, lifted up her paint-brush, and, shutting one eye, returned in silence to her measurements—"now, Elsie, let us have further details of this proposed expedition of yours. How many little Brogi shall you be required to teach?"

"There is only one pupil, and she is eighteen," I answered; "just three years younger than I."

"And you are to instruct her in all the 'ologies?"

Rosalind had taken a chair at the table, and, her head resting on her hand, was interrogating me in her quick, eager, half-ironical fashion.

"No; Mrs. Grey only says English and music. She says, too, that they are one of the principal families of Pisa. And they live in a palace," I added, with a certain satisfaction.

"It sounds quite too delightful and romantic; if it were not for Hubert, as I said before, I should insist on going myself. Pisa, the Leaning Tower, Shelley—a Marchesa in an old, ancestral palace!" And Rosalind's dark eyes shone as she spoke.

"Ruskin says that the Leaning Tower is the only ugly one in Italy," said Jenny, not moving her eyes from the Japanese pot, cleft orange, and coral necklace which she was painting.

"But the cathedral is one of the most beautiful, and the place is a mine of historical associations," answered Rosalind, her ardour not in the least damped by this piece of information.

As for me, I sat silent between these two enthusiasts with an abashed consciousness of the limitations of my own subjective feminine nature. It was neither the beauties or defects of Pisan architecture which at present occupied my mind, nor even the historical associations of the town. My thoughts dwelt solely, it must be owned, on the probable character of the human beings among whom I was to be thrown. But then it was I who was going to Pisa, and not my sisters.

"Does Mrs. Grey know the Marchesa Brogi personally?" asked my mother, who also was disposed to take the less abstract view of the matter.

"Oh, no, it is all arranged through the friend of a friend."

"I don't like the idea of your going so far, alone among strangers," sighed mother; "but, on the other hand, a change is just what you want."

"What a pity Hubert is not here tonight—that horrid *première* at the Lyceum! We must lay the plan before him tomorrow," struck in Rosalind, who, hopeless blue-stocking as she was, consulted her oracle with all the faith of a woman who barely knows how to spell.

I went over to my mother and took the stool at her feet which my sister had just vacated.

"It's going to be: 'Yes,' mother; I have felt it all along."

"My dear, I won't be the one to keep you back. But need you make up your mind so soon?"

"Mrs. Grey says that the sooner I can leave the better. They would like me to start in a week or ten days," I answered, suppressing as best I could all signs of the feeling of desolation that came over me at the sound of my own words.

"You will have to get clothes," cried Rosalind; "those little mouse-coloured garments of yours will never do for ancestral palaces."

"Oh, with some new boots and an ulster—I'm afraid I must have an ulster—I shall be quite set up."

"You would pay very well for good dressing," observed Jenny, contemplating me with her air of impartial criticism. "You have a nice figure, and a pretty head, and you know how to walk."

"'Praise from Sir Hubert Stanley,'" replied Rosalind with some irony. "My dear Elsie, I have seen it in your eyes—they are highly respectable eyes, by the bye—I have seen it in your eyes from the first moment the letter came, that you meant to go. It is you quiet women who have all the courage, if you will excuse a truism."

"Well, yes, perhaps I did feel like going from the first."

"And, now that is decided, let me tell you, Elsie, that I perfectly hate the idea of losing you," cried Rosalind with sudden abruptness; then, changing her tone, she went on—"for who knows how or when we shall have you back again? You will descend upon that *palazzo* resplendent in the new boots and the new ulster; the combined radiance of those two adornments will be too much for some Italian Mr. Rochester who, of course, will be lurking about the damask-hung corridors with their painted ceilings. Jane Eyre will be retained as a fixture, and her native land shall know her no more."

"You forget that Jane Eyre would have some voice in the matter. And I have always considered Mr. Rochester the most unpleasant person that ever a woman made herself miserable over," I answered calmly enough, for I was accustomed to these little excursions into the realms of fancy on the part of my sister.

"I think there's a little stone, Elsie, where the heart ought to be," and Rosalind, bending forward, poked her finger, with unscientific vagueness, at the left side of my waist.

"'Men have died and worms have eaten them, but not for love,'" I quoted, while there flashed across my mind a vision of Rosalind sobbing helplessly on the floor a month before Hubert proposed to her.

"*Men*; it doesn't say anything about women," answered Rosalind, thoughtfully flying off, as usual, at a tangent.

"Is it woman's mission to die of a broken heart?" I could not resist saying, for there had been some very confidential passages between us, once upon a time. "The headache is too noble for my sex; you think the heartache would sound pleasanter."

"Elsie talking women's rights!" cried Jenny, looking up astonished from her work.

"Yes; the effects of a daring and adventurous enterprise are beginning to tell upon her in advance."

"We have wandered a long way from Pisa," I said; "but that is the worst of engaged people. Whatever the conversation is, they manage to turn it into sentimental channels."

"I sentimental!" cried Rosalind, opening wide her eyes; "I, who unite in my own person the charms of Cornelia Blimber and Mrs. Jellaby, to be accused of sentiment!"

I lay awake that night on my little iron bed long after Rosalind was sleeping the sleep of happy labour. I was a coward at heart, though I had contrived to show a brave front to my little world.

At the thought of that coming plunge into the unknown, my spirit grew frozen within me, and I began to wish that the fateful letter from Mrs. Grey had never been written.

II

A Great Event

A bout ten days after the conversation recorded in the last chapter, I was driving down to Victoria station in a four-wheel cab, wearing the new ulster, the new boots, and holding on my knee a brand-new travelling-bag. It was a colourless London morning, neither hot nor cold, but as I looked out with rather dim eyes through the dirty windows, I experienced no pleasure at the thought of exchanging for Italian skies this dear, familiar greyness. At my side sat my mother, silent and pale. Now that we two were alone together—my busy sisters had been at work some hours ago—we had abandoned the rather strained and feverish gaiety which had prevailed that morning at breakfast.

"Now, Elsie, keep warm at night; don't forget to eat plenty of Brand's essence of beef—it's the brown parcel, not the white one—and write directly you arrive."

Between us we had succeeded in taking my ticket and registering the luggage, and now my mother stood at the door of the carriage, exchanging with me those last farewells which always seem so much too long and so much too short.

It must be owned, this journey of mine bore to us both the aspect of a great event. We had always been poor, most of our friends were poor, and we were not familiarized with the easy modern notions of travel, which make nothing of a visit to the North Pole, or a little trip to China by way of Peru. And as the train steamed out at last from the station my heart sank suddenly within me, and I could scarcely see the black-clothed familiar figure on the platform, for the tears which sprang to my eyes blinded me.

My first new experience was not a pleasant one, and as I lay moaning with sickness in a second-class cabin, I wondered how I or any one else could ever have complained of anything while we stood on *terra firma*. All past worries and sorrows faded momentarily into nothingness before this present all-engulfing evil. It seemed an age before we reached Calais, where, limp, bewildered, and miserable, I was jostled into a crowded second-class carriage *en route* for Basle. The train jolted and shook, and I grew more and more unhappy, mentally and physically, with every minute. My fellow-passengers, a sorry, battered-looking assortment of women, produced large untempting supplies of food from their travelling-bags, and fell to with good appetite. I myself, after some hesitation, sought consolation in the little tin of Brand's essence; after which, squeezed in between the window and a perfectly unclassifiable specimen of Englishwoman, I fell asleep.

When I awoke it was broad daylight, and the train was gliding slowly into the station at Basle.

I was stiff, cramped, and dishevelled, but yesterday's depression had given place to a new, delicious feeling of excitement. The porters hurrying to and fro, and shouting in their guttural Swiss-German, the people standing on the platform, the unfamiliar advertisements and announcements posted and painted about the station, all appeared to me objects of surpassing interest. The glamour of strangeness lay over all. A keen exhilarating morning breeze blew from the mountains, and as I stepped on to the platform it seemed as if I trod on air. With a feeling of adventure, which I firmly believe Columbus himself could never have experienced more keenly, I made my way into the crowded refreshment-room, and ordered breakfast. I was very hungry, and thought that I had never tasted anything better than the coffee and rolls, the shavings of white butter, and the adulterated honey in its little glass pot. As I sat there contentedly I found it difficult to realize that less than twenty-four hours separated me from the familiar life at Islington. It seemed incredible that so short a space of time had sufficed to land me on this strange sea of new experiences, into this dream-like, disorganized life, where night was scarcely divided from day, and the common incident of a morning meal could induce, of itself, a dozen new sensations. The rest of that day was unmixed delight. I scarcely moved my eyes from the window as the train sped on through the St. Gothard pass into Italy. What a wondrous panorama unrolled itself before me!

First, the mysterious, silent world of mountains, all black and white, like a photograph, with here and there the still, green waters of a mighty lake; the gentler scenes—trees, meadows, villages; last of all, the wide, blue waters of the Italian lakes, with their fringe of purple hills, and the little white villas clustered round them, and the red, red sunset reflected on their surfaces.

The train was late, and I missed the express at Genoa, passing several desolate hours in the great deserted station. It was not till eleven o'clock the next morning that a tired, dishevelled, and decidedly dirty young woman found herself standing on the platform at Pisa, her travelling rug trailing ignominiously behind her as she held out her luggage check in dumb entreaty to a succession of unresponsive porters.

The pleasant excitement of yesterday had faded, and I was conscious of being exceedingly tired and rather forlorn. Here was no exhilarating mountain air, but a damp breeze, at once chilly and enervating, made me shiver where I stood.

I succeeded at last, in spite of a complete absence of Italian, in conveying myself and my luggage into a fly, and in directing the driver to the Palazzo Brogi. As we jolted along slowly enough, I looked out, expecting every minute to see the Leaning Tower; but I saw only tall, grey streets, narrow and often without sidewalks, in which a sparse but picturesque population was moving to and fro. But I was roused, tired as I was, to considerable interest as we crossed the bridge, and my eye took in the full sweep of the river, with the noble curve of palaces along its bank, the distant mountains, beautiful in the sunshine, and the clear and delicate light which lay over all.

I had not long, however, to observe these things, for in another minute the drosky had stopped before a great square house in grey stone, with massive iron scrolls guarding the lower windows, and the driver, coming to the door, announced that this was the Palazzo Brogi.

My heart sank as I dismounted, and going up the steps, pulled timidly at the bell. The great door was standing open, and I could see beyond into a gloomy and cavernous vista of corridors.

No one answered the bell, but just as I was about to pull for the second time a gentleman, dressed in a grey morning suit *à l'anglais*, strolled out inquiringly into the passage. He was rather stout, of middle height, with black hair parted in the middle, and a pale, good-looking face. The fact that no one had answered the bell seemed neither to disconcert nor surprise him; he called out a few words in Italian, and, advancing towards me, bowed with charming courtesy.

"You are Miss Meredith," he said, speaking in English, slowly, with difficulty, but in the softest voice in the world; "my mother did not expect you by the early train." Here his English seemed to break down suddenly, and he looked at me a moment with his dark and gentle eyes. There was something reassuring in his serious, simple dignity of manner; I forgot my fears, forgot also the fact that I was as black as a coal, and had lost nearly all my hair-pins, and said, composedly, "I missed the express from Genoa. The train across the St. Gothard was late."

At this point there emerged from the shadowy region at the back a servant in livery, who very deliberately, and without explanation of his tardiness, proceeded to help the driver in carrying my box into the hall.

The gentleman bowed himself away, and in another moment I was following the servant up a vast and interminable flight of stone stairs.

The vaulted roof rose high above us, half lost to sight in shadow; everywhere were glimpses of galleries and corridors, and over everything hung that indescribable atmosphere of chill stuffiness which I have since learned to connect with Italian palaces.

Anything less homelike, less suggestive of a place where ordinary human beings carried on the daily, pleasant avocations of life, it would be impossible to conceive. A stifling sensation rose in my throat as we passed through a folding glass-door, across a dim corridor, into a large room, where my guide left me with a remark which of course I did not understand. With a sense of unutterable relief I perceived the room to be empty, and I sat down on a yellow damask sofa, feeling an ignominious desire to cry. The shutters were closed before the great windows, but through the gloom I could see that the place was furnished very stiffly with yellow damask furniture, while enormous and elaborate chests and writing-tables filled up the corners. A big chandelier shrouded in yellow muslin hung from the ceiling, which rose to a great height, and was painted in fresco. There was no fire, and I looked at the empty gilt stove, which had neither bars nor fire-irons, with a shiver.

It was not long before an inner door was thrown open to admit two ladies, who came towards me with greetings in French. The Marchesa Brogi was a small, vivacious, dried-up woman of middle age, with an evident sense of her own dignity, looking very cold and carrying a little muff in her hands.

She curtseyed slightly as we shook hands, then motioned me to a seat beside her on the sofa. "This is my daughter Bianca," she said, turning to the girl who had followed her into the room.

I looked anxiously at my pupil, whose aspect was not altogether reassuring. She was a tall, pale, high-shouldered young person, elaborately dressed, with a figure so artificially bolstered up that only by a great stretch of imagination could one realize that she was probably built on average anatomical lines. Her hair, dressed on the top of her head and struck through with tortoiseshell combs, produced by its unnatural neatness the same effect of unreality. She was decidedly plain withal, and her manners struck me as being inferior to those of her mother and brother. She took up her seat at some little distance from the sofa, and whenever I glanced in her direction, I saw a pair of sharp eyes fixed on my face, with something of the unsparing criticism of a hostile child in their gaze.

I began to be terribly conscious of my disordered appearance—I am not one of those people who can afford to affect the tempestuous petticoat—and grew more and more bewildered in my efforts to follow the little Marchesa through the mazes of her fluent but curiously accentuated French.

It was with a feeling of relief that I saw one of the inner doors open, and a stout, good-tempered looking lady, in a loose morning jacket, come smiling into the room. She shook hands with me cordially, and taking a chair opposite the sofa, began to nod and smile in the most reassuring fashion. She spoke no English and very little French, but was determined that so slight an obstacle should not stand in the way of pressing her goodwill towards me.

I began to like this fat, silly lady, who showed her gums so unbecomingly when she smiled, and to wonder at her position in the household.

The door opened yet again, and in came my first acquaintance, the gentleman in the grey suit.

I was growing more and more confused with each fresh arrival, and dimly wondered how long it would be before I fell off the hard yellow sofa from sheer weariness. The strange faces surged before me, an indistinguishable mass; the strange voices reached me, meaningless and incoherent, through a thick veil.

"She is very tired," someone said in French; and not long after this I was led across half a dozen rooms to a great bedroom, where, without taking in any details of my surroundings, I undressed, went to bed, and fell asleep till the next morning.

III

New and Strange Experiences

When I awoke the sun was streaming in through the chinks of the shutters, and a servant was standing at my bedside with a cup of coffee and some rolls. But I felt no disposition to attack my breakfast, and lay still, with a dreamy sensation as my eyes wandered round the unfamiliar room.

I saw a great, dim chamber, with a painted ceiling rising sky-high above me; plaster walls, coarsely stencilled in arabesques; a red-tiled floor, strewn here and there with squares of carpet; a few old and massive pieces of furniture, and not the vestige of a stove. The bed on which I lay was a vast four-post structure, mountains high, with a baldaquin in faded crimson damask, and was reflected, rather libellously, in a glass-front of a wardrobe opposite.

"I shall never, never feel that it is a normal, human bedroom," I thought, appalled by the gloomy state of my surroundings. Then I drank my coffee, and, climbing out of bed, went across to the window, and unshuttered it.

An exclamation of pleasure rose to my lips at the sight which greeted me.

Below flowed the full waters of the Arno, spanned by a massive bridge of shining white marble, and reflecting on its waves the bluest of blue heavens. A brilliant and delicate sunshine was shed over all, bringing out the lights and shades, the differences of tint and surface, of the tall old house on the opposite bank, and falling on the minute spires of a white marble church perched at the very edge of the stream.

The sight of this toy-like structure—surely the smallest and daintiest place of worship in the world—served to deepen the sense of unreality which was hourly gaining hold upon me.

"I wonder where the Leaning Tower is," I thought, as I hastily drew on my stockings, for standing about on the red-tiled floor had made me very cold, in spite of the sunshine flooding in through the windows; "what would they say at home if they heard I had been twenty-four hours in Pisa without so much as seeing it in the distance."

But I did not allow myself to think of home, and devoted my energies to bringing myself up to the high standard of neatness which would certainly be expected of me.

I found the ladies sitting together in a large and cold apartment, which was more homelike than the yellow room of yesterday, inasmuch as its bareness was relieved by a variety of modern ornaments, photograph-frames, and other trifles, all as hideous as your latter-day Italian loves to make them. They greeted me with ceremony, making many polite inquiries as to my health and comfort, and invited me to sit down. The room was very cold, in spite of the morning sun, whose light, moreover, was intercepted by venetian blinds. The chilly little Marchesa had her hands in her muff, while her daughter warmed hers over a *scaldino*, a small earthern pot filled with hot wood ashes, which she held in her lap.

The amiable lady in the dressing-jacket was evidently a more warm-blooded creature, for she stitched on, undaunted by the cold, at a large and elaborate piece of embroidery, taking her part meanwhile in the ceaseless and rapid flow of chatter.

It was rather a shock to me to gather that she was the wife of the charming son of the house; to whom, moreover, a fresh charm was added, when it came out that his name was Romeo. I had put her down for a woman of middle age, but I learned subsequently that she was only twenty-eight years old, and had brought her husband a very handsome dowry. The pair were childless after several years of marriage, and they lived permanently at the Palazzo Brogi, according to the old patriarchal Italian custom, which, like most old customs, is dying out.

I sat there, stupidly wondering if I should ever be able to understand Italian, replying lamely enough to the remarks in French which were thrown out to me at decent intervals, and encountering every now and then with some alarm the suspicious glances of the Signorina Bianca.

Once the kind Marchesina Annunziata—Romeo's wife—drew my attention with simple pride to a leather chair embroidered with gold, her own handiwork, as I managed to make out.

I smiled and nodded the proper amount of admiration, and wished secretly that my feet were not so cold, for the tiled floor struck chill through the carpet. Bianca offered me a scaldino presently, and the Marchesa explained that she wished the English lessons to begin on the following day. After that I sat there in almost unbroken silence till twelve o'clock, when the casual man-servant strolled in and announced that lunch was ready.

The dining-room, a large and stony apartment with a vaulted roof, was situated on the ground-floor, and here we found the Marchesino Romeo and the old Marchese, to whom I was introduced. The meal was slight but excellently cooked; and the sweet Tuscan wine I found delicious. Romeo, who sat next to me, and attended to my wants with his air of gentle and serious courtesy, addressed a few remarks to me in English and then subsided into a graceful silence, leaving the conversation entirely in the hands of his womenkind.

After lunch, a drive and round of calls was proposed by the ladies, who invited me to join them. The thought of being shut up in a carriage with these three strange women, all speaking their unknown tongue, was too much for me, and gathering courage, the courage of desperation, I announced that unless my services were required I should prefer to go for a walk.

The ladies looked at me, and then at one another, and the good-natured Annunziata burst into a laugh. "It is an English custom," she explained. "You must not go beyond the city walls, Miss Meredith, not even into the Casine; it would not be safe," said the Marchesa; while Bianca looked scrutinizingly at my square, low-heeled shoes which contrasted sharply with her own.

It was with a feeling of relief, some twenty minutes later, that, peeping from the window of my room, I saw them all drive off, elaborately apparelled, in a closed carriage; Romeo, bareheaded, speeding them from the steps.

Then I sat down and wrote off an unnaturally cheerful letter to the people at home, only pausing now and then when the tears rose to my eyes and blurred my sight.

"I hope I haven't overdone it," I thought, as I addressed the envelope and proceeded to dress. "I'm not sure that there isn't a slightly inebriated tone about the whole thing, and mother is so quick at reading between the lines."

I passed across the corridor and down the stair to the first landing, where I lingered a moment. A covered gallery ran along the back of the house, and through the tall and dingy windows I could see a surging, unequal mass of old red roofs.

"How Jenny would love it all," I thought, as I turned away with a sigh.

As I reached the street door, Romeo emerged from that mysterious retreat of his on the ground-floor, where he appeared to pass his time in some solitary pursuit, looked at me, bowed, and withdrew.

"At last!" I cried, inwardly, as I sped down the steps. At last I could breathe again, at last I was out in the sunlight and in the wind, away from the musty chilliness, the lurking shadows of that stifling palace. Oh, the joy of freedom and of solitude! Was it only hours? Surely it must be years that I had been imprisoned behind those thick old walls and iron guarded windows. On, on I went with rapid foot in the teeth of the biting wind and the glare of the scorching sunlight, scarcely noticing my surroundings in the first rapture of recovered freedom. But by degrees the strangeness, the beauty of what I saw, began to assert themselves.

I had turned off from the Lung' Arno, and was threading my way among the old and half-deserted streets which led to the cathedral.

What a dead, world-forgotten place, and yet how beautiful in its desolation! Everywhere were signs of a present poverty, everywhere of a past magnificence.

The men with their sombreros and cloaks worn toga fashion; their handsome, melancholy faces and stately gait; the women bareheaded, graceful, drawing water from the fountain into copper vessels, moved before me like figures from an old-world drama.

Here and there was a little, empty piazza, the tall houses abutting on it at different angles, without sidewalks, the grass growing up between the stones. It seemed only waiting for first gentleman and second gentleman to come forward and carry on their dialogue while the great "set" was being prepared at the back of the stage.

The old walls, roughly patched with modern brick and mortar, had bits of exquisite carving imbedded in them like fossils; and at every street corner the house leek sprang from the interstices of a richly wrought moulding. A great palace, with a wonderful façade, had been turned into a wineshop; and the chestnut-sellers dispensed their wares in little gloomy caverns hollowed out beneath the abodes of princes. Already the nameless charm of Italy was beginning to work on me; that magic spell from which—let us once come under its influence—we can never hope to be released.

A long and straggling street led me at last to the Piazzi del Duomo, and here for a moment I paused breathless, regardless of the icy blast which swept across from the sea.

I thought then, and I think still, that nowhere in the world is there anything which, in its own way, can equal the picture that greeted my astonished vision.

The wide and straggling grass-grown piazza, bounded on one side by the city wall, on the other by the low wall of the Campo Santo, with the wind whistling drearily across it, struck me as the very type and symbol of desolation.

At one end rose the Leaning Tower, pallid, melancholy, defying the laws of nature in a disappointingly spiritless fashion. Close against it the magnificent bulk of the cathedral reared itself, a marvel of mellow tints, of splendid outline, and richly modelled surfaces. And, divided from this by a strip of rank grass, up sprang the little quaint baptistery, with its extraordinary air of freshness and of fantastic gaiety, looking as though it had been turned out of a mould the day before yesterday.

Such richness, such forlornness, struck curiously on the sense. It was as though, wandering along some solitary shore, one had found a heaped treasure glittering undisturbed on the open sand.

I strolled for sometime spell-bound about the cathedral, not caring to multiply impressions by entering, shivering a little in the wind which held a recollection of the sea, and was at the same time cold and feverish. By and by, however, I made my way into the Campo Santo, lingering fascinated in those strange sculptured arcades, with the visions of life and death, and hell and heaven, painted on the walls.

One or two cypresses rose from the little grass-plot in the middle, and in the rank grass the jonquils were already in flower. I plucked a few of these and fastened them in my dress. They had a sweet, peculiar odour, melancholy, enervating.

The bright light was beginning to fail as I sped back hurriedly through the streets.

It was Epiphany, and the children were blowing on long glass trumpets. Every now and then the harsh sound echoed through the stony thoroughfare. It fell upon my overwrought senses like a sound of doom. The flowers in my bodice smelt of death; there was death, I thought, crying out in every old stone of the city.

The palazzo looked almost like home, and I fled up the dim stairs with a greater feeling of relief than that with which an hour or two ago I had hastened down them.

After dinner the Marchesa received her friends in the yellow drawing-room.

A wood fire was lighted on the flat, open hearth of the stove, and a side table was spread with a few light refreshments—a bottle of Marsala wine, and a round cake covered with bright green sugar, being the most important items.

About eight o'clock the visitors began to arrive, and in half an hour nine or ten ladies and three or four gentlemen were clustered on the damask sofas, talking at a great rate, and gesticulating in their graceful, eager fashion. Bianca had withdrawn into a corner with a pair of contemporaries, whose long, stiff waists, high-heeled shoes, and elaborately dressed hair, resembled her own. The old Marchese sat apart, silent and contemplative, as was his wont, and Romeo, drawing a chair close to mine, questioned me in his precise, restricted English as to my afternoon walk.

This parliament of gossip, which, as I afterwards discovered, occurred regularly three times a week, was prolonged till midnight, but, kind Annunziata noticing my tired looks, I was able to make my escape by ten o'clock.

As I climbed into my bed, worn out by the crowded experiences of the day, there rose before me suddenly a vision of the parlour at home; of mother sewing by the fireside; of Jenny and Rosalind at work in the lamplight; of Hubert coming in with the evening papers and bits of literary gossip.

"If they could only see me," I thought, "alone in this unnatural place, with no one to be fond of me, with no one even being aware that I have a Christian name."

This last touch struck me as so pathetic that the tears began to pour down my face. But the tall bed, with the faded baldaquin, if oppressive to the imagination, was, it must be confessed, exceedingly comfortable, and it was not long before I forgot my troubles in sleep.

IV

The New Governess and her Pupil

The English lesson next morning proved rather an ordeal. It took place in one of the many sitting-rooms, a large room with an open hearth, on which, however, no fire was lighted. But with a shawl round my shoulders, and a *casseta*, or brass box filled with live charcoal, for my feet, I managed to keep moderately warm.

Bianca rather sullenly drew a small collection of reading-books, grammars, and exercise-books, all bearing marks of careless usage, from a cabinet, and placed them on the table. Then drawing a chair opposite mine, she fixed her suspicious, curious eyes on me, and said in French—

"Have you any sisters, Miss Meredith?"

"I have two. But we must speak English, Marchesina."

"I always spoke French with Miss Clarke," answered Bianca.

Miss Clarke, as I subsequently gathered, was my predecessor, who had recently left the palazzo after a sojourn of eighteen months, and who, to judge by results, must have performed her duties in a singularly perfunctory fashion.

"Are your sisters married?" Bianca condescended to say in English, looking critically at my grey merino gown, with its banded bodice, and at my hair braided simply round my head.

"No; but one is engaged."

"And have you any brothers?"

"No; not one."

"And I have not one sister, and two brothers, signorina," cried Bianca, apparently much struck by the contrast. "It is my brother Andrea who is so anxious for me to learn and to read books, although I am past eighteen. He writes about it to my father, and my father always does what Andrea tells him."

"Then you must work hard to please your brother," I said, with my most didactic air, examining the well-thumbed English-Italian grammar as I spoke.

"What is the use, when he has been five years in America? Who knows when I may see him? Ah! *molto indipendente* is Andrea—*molto indipendente!*" And Bianca shook her too-neat head with a sigh of mingled pride and approbation.

We made a little attack on the grammars and reading-books in the course of the morning, but it was uphill work, and I sat down to the piano, feeling thoroughly disheartened.

But the music lesson was a great improvement on the English. Bianca had some taste, and considerable power of execution, and we rose from the piano better friends. A short walk before lunch was prescribed by the Marchesa, and soon I was re-threading the mazes of the Pisa streets, Bianca hobbling slowly and discontentedly at my side on her high heels.

My pupil's one idea with regard to a walk was shops, and now she announced her intention of buying some *torino*, the sweet paste of honey and almonds so dear to Italian palates. As we turned into the narrow street, with its old, old houses and stone arcades, where, such as they are, the principal shops of Pisa are to be found, I could not suppress an exclamation of delight at the sight of so much picturesqueness.

"Ah," said Bianca, not in the least understanding my enthusiasm; "you should see the shops at Turin, and the great squares, and the glass arcades, and the wide streets. I have been there twice. Romeo says it is almost as beautiful as Paris."

The ladies drove out again after lunch in the closed carriage, and again I set out alone to explore the town. This time I penetrated into the interior of the cathedral, spending two happy hours in the dusky richness of the vast building; lost in admiration, now of the soft rich colour of marble and jasper and painted glass; now of the pictures on walls, roof, and altar; now of the grandeur of line, the mysterious effects of light and shadow planned by the cunning brain of a long departed master.

The weather was much milder than on the previous day, and half a dozen tourists, with red guide-books, were making a round of inspection of the buildings on the piazza.

Two of these I recognized with a thrill to be my own compatriots. They were, to the outward eye, at least, quite uninteresting; a bride and bridegroom, presumably, of the most commonplace type; but I followed them about the cathedral with a lingering, wistful glance which I am sure, had they been conscious of it, would have melted them to pity. Once, as I was standing before Andrea del Sarto's marvellous St. Catherine, the pair came up behind me.

"It's like your sister Nellie," said the man.

"Nonsense! Nellie isn't half so fat, and she never did her hair like that in her life. Why, you wouldn't know Nellie without her fringe," answered the woman in a superior way as they moved off to the next object of interest mentioned in Baedecker.

They were Philistines, no doubt; but I was in no mood to be critical, and must confess that the sound of their English voices was almost too much for my self-control.

The ladies went out after dinner, and I was left to the pains and pleasures of a solitary evening, an almost unprecedented experience in my career. The next day was Sunday: the family drove to early mass, and an hour or two later I made my way to the English church, the sparseness of whose congregation gave it rather a forlorn aspect.

The English colony is small, and consists chiefly of invalids attracted by the mildness of the climate, who at the same time are too poor to seek a more fashionable health resort.

They did not, as may be imagined, present a very cheerful aspect, but the sight of them filled me with a passing envy. Mothers and daughters, sisters, friends; everyone came in in groups or pairs, with the exception of myself; I, the most friendless and forlorn of all these exiles.

The chaplain and his wife called on me after I had sent in my name for a sitting, but there was never much intimacy between us.

In the evening of this, my first Sunday away from home, the Marchesa again "received," and once more I sat bewildered amid the flood of unintelligible chatter, or exchanged occasional remarks with Bianca, who appeared to have abandoned her suspicions of me, and had taken up her place at my side.

V

MAKING FRIENDS

I bought a dictionary and a grammar, and worked hard in my moments of leisure. My daily life, moreover, might be described as an almost unbroken Italian lesson, and it was not long before I began to understand what was said around me, and to express myself more or less haltingly in the language of my land of exile. A means of communication being thus opened up between myself and the Marchesina Annunziata, that open-hearted person began to take me into her confidence, and to pour out for my benefit a dozen little facts and circumstances which I might have lived all my life with the voluble, but reserved, Marchesa without ever having learnt.

Of Andrea, the absent son, she spoke often.

"Molto indipendente!" she said shaking her head, and using the same expression as her young sister-in-law.

This reprobate, it seemed, flying in the face of family tradition, had announced from the first his intention of earning his own living; had studied hard and with distinction for a civil engineer, and five years ago, refusing all offers of help, had accepted a post in America.

As for Romeo, the elder brother, he also, said his wife, was very clever; had passed his examinations as a barrister. "But, of course," she added, with naïve pride, "he would never think of practising."

Romeo, indeed, to do him justice, was troubled by no disturbing spirit of radicalism, and carried on the ancestral pursuit of doing nothing with a grace and a persistence which one could not help but admire.

His mother possessed a fine natural aptitude for the same branch of industry; but the old Marchese, whom, though he spoke but little and was seldom seen, I soon perceived to have a character of his own, passed his days in reading and writing in some obscure retreat on the ground-floor.

Bianca, after suspending her judgment for some days, had apparently given a verdict in my favour, for she now followed me about like a dog, a line of conduct which, though flattering, had certainly its drawbacks. The English lessons were always a trial, but they grew better as time went on, and the music lessons were far more satisfactory.

As for me, I began to grow fond of my pupil; she was such a crude, instinctive creature, so curiously undeveloped for her time of life, that one could not but take her under one's wing and forgive her her failings as one forgives a little child.

I had now been a month in Pisa, and the first sense of desolation and strangeness had worn off. There were moments, even now, when the longing for home grew so desperate that I was on the point of rushing off to England by the next train; but I was growing accustomed to my surroundings; the sense of being imprisoned in an enchanted palace had vanished, and had been followed by a more prosaic, but more comfortable, adaptation to environment.

My life moved from day to day in a groove, and I ceased to question the order of things. In the morning were the lessons and the walk with Bianca; the afternoons were looked upon as my own, and these I generally passed in reading, writing letters, and in walking about the city, whose every stone I was getting to know by heart.

Often leaning on the bridge and looking across at the palaces curving along the river, I peopled with a visionary company the lofty rooms beyond the lofty windows.

Here Shelley came with his wife and the Williams', and here it was that they made acquaintance with Emilia Vivian, the heroine of "Epipsychidion." Byron had a palazzo all to himself, whence he rode out with Trelawney, to the delight of the population.

Leigh Hunt lingered here in his many wanderings, and Landor led a hermit life in some hidden corner of the old town.

Claire Clairmont, that unfortunate mortal, who where'er she came brought calamity, vibrated discontentedly between here and Florence, and it seemed that sometimes I saw her, a little, unhappy, self-conscious ghost, looking from the upper windows of Shelley's palace.

And here, too, after the storm and the shipwreck in which their lives' happiness had gone down, came those two forlorn women, Mary Shelley and Jane Williams. Upon the picture of such sorrow I could not trust myself to gaze; only now and then I heard their shadowy weeping in some dim, great chamber of a half-deserted house.

At other times, I returned to my first friend, the great piazza, whose marvels it seemed impossible to exhaust, and for which I grew to entertain a curiously personal affection.

But as the spring came on, and the mild, enervating breezes ousted more and more their colder comrades, I began to long with all my soul and body for the country. The brown hills, so near and yet so far, inspired me with a fervour of longing. I had promised never to go beyond the city walls; even the great park, or Casine, where already the trees were burgeoning, was forbidden ground, though sometimes, indeed, I drove out there with the ladies. The cool and distant peaks of the Apennines drew my heart towards them with an ever-growing magnetism.

The cypresses and ilexes springing up beyond the high white walls of a garden, the scent of spring flowers borne across to me in passing, filled me with a longing and a melancholy which were new to me.

As a matter of fact, the enervating climate, the restricted life and the solitude—for solitude, when all were said, it was—were beginning to tell upon my health. I was not unhappy, but I grew thin and pale, and was developing a hitherto unknown mood of dreamy introspection.

In June, I gathered, the whole Brogi household would adjourn to the family villa near the baths of Lucca. It was taken for granted that I was to accompany them, and, indeed, I had determined on making out my full year, should my services be required for so long.

After that, no doubt, a husband would be found for Bianca, and I could return to England with a clear conscience and quite a nice little amount of savings. Mother should have a deep arm-chair, and Rosalind a really handsome wedding present; and with my new acquisition of Italian I hoped to be able to command a higher price in the educational market.

The evenings were generally passed in chatter, in which I soon learnt to take my part; and I began to be included in the invitations to the houses of the various ladies who "received," like the Marchesa, on certain evenings of the week.

No subject of gossip was too trivial for discussion; and I could not but admire the way in which the tiniest incident was taken up, turned inside out, battledored this way and that, and finally wore threadbare before it was allowed to drop, by these highly skilled talkers. Talk, indeed, was the business of their lives, the staple fare of existence.

Everyone treated me with perfect courtesy, but also, it must be owned, with perfect coldness.

Bianca, as I said before, developed a sort of fondness for me; and Annunziata included me in her general benevolence—Annunziata, good soul, who was always laughing, when she was not deluged in tears. I fancy the charming Romeo had his drawbacks as a husband.

The Marchesa, with her glib talk, her stately courtesy, was in truth the chilliest and the most reserved of mortals. Of Romeo I saw but little. With the old Marchese, alone, I was conscious of a silent sympathy.

VI

COSTANZA MARCHETTI

O ne morning after breakfast I found the whole family assembled in the yellow drawing-room in a state of unusual excitement. Even the bloodless little Marchesa had a red spot on either shrivelled cheek, and her handsome old husband had thrown off for once his mask of impenetrable and impassive dignity in favour of an air of distinct and lively pleasure.

Bianca was chattering, Romeo was smiling, and Annunziata, of course, was smiling too. Beckoning me confidentially towards her, and showing her gums even more freely than usual, she said: "There is great news. The Marchesino Andrea is coming home. We have had a letter this morning, and we are to expect him within a fortnight."

I received with genuine interest this piece of information. From the first I had decided that the rebel was probably the most interesting member of his family, and had even gone so far as to "derive" him from his father, in accordance with the latter-day scientific fashion which has infected the most unscientific among us.

Bianca was quite unmanageable that morning, and I had finally to abandon all attempts at discipline and let her chat away, in English, to her heart's content.

"I cried all day when Andrea went away," she rattled on; "I was quite a little thing, and I did nothing but cry. Even mamma cried, too. When he was home she was often very, very angry with Andrea. Everyone was always being angry with him," she added presently, "but everyone liked him best. There was often loud talking with papa and Romeo. I used to peep from the door of my nursery and see Andrea stride past with a white face and a great frown." She knitted her own pale brows together in illustration of her own words, and looked so ridiculous that I could not help laughing.

I judged it best, moreover, to cut short these confidences, and we adjourned, with some reluctance on her part, to the piano.

Lunch was a very cheerful meal that day, and afterwards Bianca thrust her arm in mine and dragged me gaily up to the sitting-room.

"Only think," she said, "mamma is writing to Costanza Marchetti at Florence to ask her to stay with us the week after next."

"Is the signorina a great friend of yours?"

Bianca looked exceedingly sly. "Oh yes, she is a great friend of mine. I stayed with her once at Florence. They have a beautiful, beautiful house on the Lung' Arno, and Costanza has more dresses than she can wear."

She spoke with such an air of naïve and important self-consciousness that I could scarcely refrain from smiling.

It was impossible not to see through her meaning. The beloved truant was to be permanently trapped; the trap to be baited with a rich, perhaps a beautiful bride.

The situation was truly interesting; I foresaw the playing out of a little comedy under my very eyes. Life quickened perceptibly in the palazzo after the receipt of the letter from America.

Plans for picnics, balls, and other gaieties were freely discussed. There was a constant dragging about of heavy furniture along the corridors, from which I gathered that rooms were being suitably prepared both for Andrea and his possible bride.

At the gossip parliaments, nothing else was talked of but the coming event; the misdemeanours of servants, the rudeness of tradesmen, and the latest Pisan scandal being relegated for the time being to complete obscurity.

In about ten days Costanza Marchetti appeared on the scene.

We were sitting in the yellow drawing-room after lunch when the carriage drove up, followed by a fly heavily laden with luggage.

Bianca had rushed to the window at the sound of wheels, and had hastily described the cavalcade.

A few minutes later in came Romeo with a young, or youngish, lady, dressed in the height of fashion, on his arm.

She advanced towards the Marchesa with a sort of sliding curtsy, and shook hands from the elbow in a manner worthy of Bond Street. But the meeting between her and Bianca was even more striking.

Retreating a little, to allow free play for their operations, the young ladies tilted forward on their high heels, precipitating themselves into one another's arms, where they kissed one another violently on either cheek. Retreating again, they returned once more to the charge, and the performance was gone through for a second time.

Then they sat down close together on the sofa, stroking one another's hands.

"Costanza powders so thickly with violet powder, it makes me quite ill," Bianca confided to me later in the day; "and she thinks there is nobody like herself in all the world."

When the Contessima, for that I discovered was her style and title, had detached her fashionable bird-cage veil from the brim of her large hat, I fell to observing her with some curiosity from my modest corner. She was no longer in her first youth—about twenty-eight, I should say—but she was distinctly handsome, in a rather hard-featured fashion.

When she was introduced to me, she bowed very stiffly, and said, "How do you do, Miss?" in the funniest English I had ever heard.

"It is so good of you to come to us," said the Marchesa, with her usual stateliness; "to leave your gay Florence before the end of the Carnival for our quiet Pisa. We cannot promise you many parties and balls, Costanza."

Perhaps Costanza had seen too many balls in her time—had discovered them, perhaps (who knows?), to be merely dust and ashes.

At any rate, she eagerly and gushingly disclaimed her hostess's insinuation, and there was voluble exchange of compliments between the ladies.

"Will you give Bianca a holiday for this week, Miss Meredith?" said the Marchesa, presently.

"Certainly, if you will allow it," I answered, saying what I knew I was intended to say.

Costanza looked across at me coldly, taking in the modest details of my costume.

"And when does the Marchesino arrive?" she asked, turning to his mother.

"Not till late on Thursday night."

Bianca counted upon her fingers.

"Three whole days and a half," she cried.

"On Friday," said the Marchesa, "we have arranged a little dance. It is so near the end of Carnival we could not put it off till long after his arrival."

"Ah, dearest Marchesa," cried Costanza, clasping her hands in a rather mechanical rapture, "it will be too delightful! Do we dance in the ball-room below, or in here?"

"In the ball-room," said the Marchesa, while Annunziata nodded across at me, saying—

"Do you dance, Miss Meredith?"

"Yes; I am very fond of it," I answered, but it must be owned that I looked forward with but scant interest to the festivity. My insular mind was unable to rise to the idea of Italian partners.

Costanza raised her eyeglass, with its long tortoiseshell handle, to her heavy-lidded eyes, and surveyed me scrutinizingly. It had been evident from the first that she had but a poor opinion of me.

"I hope you will join us on Friday, Miss Meredith," said the Marchesa, with much ceremony.

I could not help feeling snubbed. I had taken it for granted that I was to appear; this formal invitation was inexpressibly chilling.

I did not enjoy my holiday of the next few days. I had always been exceedingly grateful for my few hours of daily solitude, and these were mine no more.

The fact that the ladies of the household never seemed to need either solitude or silence had impressed me from the first as a curious phenomenon. Now, for the time being, I was dragged into the current of their lives, and throughout the day was forced to share in the ceaseless chatter, without which, it seemed, a guest could not be entertained, a ball given, or even a son received into the bosom of his family.

Here, there, and everywhere was the unfortunate Miss Meredith— at everybody's beck and call, "upstairs, downstairs, and in my lady's chamber."

"It is fortunate that it is only me," I reflected. "I don't know what Jenny or Rosalind would do. They would just pack up and go." For, at home, the liberty of the individual had always been greatly respected, which was, perhaps, the reason why we managed to live together in such complete harmony.

As for Bianca and her friend, they clattered about all day long together on their high heels, their arms intertwined, exchanging confidences, comparing possessions, and eating *torino* till their teeth ached. In the intervals of this absorption in friendship my pupil would come up to me, throw her arms round me, and pour out a flood of the frankest criticisms on the fair Costanza. To these I refused to listen.

"How can I tell, Bianca, that you do not rush off to the Contessima and complain of me to her?"

"Dearest little signorina, there could be nothing to complain of."

"Of course," I said, "we know that. I am perfect. But, seriously, Bianca, I do not understand this kissing and hugging of a person one moment, and saying evil things of her the next."

Bianca was getting on for nineteen, but it was necessary to treat her like a child. She hung her head, and took the rebuke very meekly.

"But, signorina, say what you will, Costanza does put wadding in her stays because she is so thin, and then pretends to have a fine figure. And she has a bad temper, as everyone knows. . ."

"Bianca, you are incorrigible!" I put my hand across her mouth, and ran down the corridor to my own room.

VII

THE HOME-COMING OF THE REBEL

The covered gallery which ran along the back of the house was flooded in the afternoon with sunshine. Here, as the day declined, I loved to pace, basking in the warmth and rejoicing in the brightness, for mild and clear as the day might be out of doors, within the thick-walled palace it was always mirk and chill.

The long, high wall of the gallery was covered with pictures—chiefly paintings of dead and gone Brogi—most of them worthless, taken singly; taken collectively, interesting as a study of the varieties of family types.

Here was Bianca, to the life, painted two centuries ago; the old Marchese looked out from a dingy canvass 300 years old at least, and a curious mixture of Romeo and his sister disported itself in powder amid a florid eighteenth century family group. Conspicuous among so much indifferent workmanship hung a genuine Bronzino of considerable beauty, representing a young man, whose charming aspect was scarcely marred by his stiff and elaborate fifteenth century costume. The dark eyes of this picture had a way of following one up and down the gallery in a rather disconcerting manner; already I had woven a series of little legends about him, and had decided that he left his frame at night, like the creatures in "Ruddygore," to roam the house as a ghost where once he had lived as a man.

Opposite the pictures, on which they shed their light, was a row of windows, set close together deep in the thick wall, and rising almost to the ceiling. They were not made open, but through their numerous and dingy panes I could see across the roofs of the town to the hills, or down below to where a neglected bit of territory, enclosed between high walls, did duty as a garden.

In one corner of this latter stood a great ilex tree, its massive grey trunk old and gnarled, its blue-green foliage casting a wide shadow. Two or three cypresses, with their broom-like stems, sprang from the overgrown turf, which, at this season of the year, was beginning to be yellow with daffodils, and a thick growth of laurel bushes ran along under the walls. An empty marble basin, approached by broken pavement, marked the site of a forgotten fountain, the stone-crop running riot about its borders; the house-leek thrusting itself every now and then through the interstices of shattered stone. Forlorn, uncared for as was this square of ground, it had for me a mysterious attraction; it seemed to me that there clung to it through all change of times and weathers, something of the beauty in desolation which makes the charm of Italy.

It was about four o'clock on Thursday afternoon, and I was wandering up and down the gallery in the sunshine.

I was alone for the first time during the last three days, and was making the best of this brief respite from the gregarious life to which I saw myself doomed for sometime to come. The ladies were out driving, paying calls and making a few last purchases for the coming festivities. In the evening Andrea was expected, and an atmosphere of excitement pervaded the whole household.

"They are really fond of him, it seems," I mused; "these people who, as far as I can make out, are so cold."

Then I leaned my forehead disconsolately against the window, and had a little burst of sadness all by myself.

The constant strain of the last few days had tired me. I longed intensely for peace, for rest, for affection, for the sweet and simple kindliness of home.

I had even lost my interest in the coming event which seemed to accentuate my forlornness.

What were other people's brothers to me? Let mother or one of the girls come out to me, and I would not be behindhand in rejoicing. "No one wants me, no one cares for me, and I don't care for any one either," I said to myself gloomily, brushing away a stray tear with the back of my hand. Then I moved from the window and my contemplation of the ilex tree, and began slowly pacing down the gallery, which was getting fuller every minute of the thick golden sunlight.

But suddenly my heart seemed to stop beating, my blood froze, loud pulses fell to throbbing in my ears. I remained rooted to the spot with horror, while my eyes fixed themselves on a figure, which, as yet on the further side of a shaft of moted sunlight, was slowly advancing towards me from the distant end of the gallery.

"Is it the Bronzino come to life?" whispered a voice in the back recess of my consciousness. The next moment I was laughing at my own fears, and was contemplating with interest and astonishment the very flesh-

and-blood presentiment of a modern gentleman which stood bowing before me.

"I fear I have startled you," said a decidedly human voice, speaking in English, with a peculiar accent, while the speaker looked straight at me with a pair of dark eyes that were certainly like those of the Bronzino.

"Oh, no; it was my own fault for being so stupid," I answered rather breathlessly, shaken out of my self-possession.

"I am Andrea Brogi," he said, with a little bow; "and I believe I have the pleasure of addressing Miss Clarke?"

"I am Miss Meredith, your sister's governess," I answered, feeling perhaps a little hurt that the substitution of one English teacher for another had not been thought a matter of sufficient importance for mention in the frequent letters which the family had been in the habit of sending to America. Andrea, with great simplicity, went on to explain his presence in the gallery.

"I am some hours before my time, you see. I had miscalculated the trains between this and Livorno. Now don't you think this a nice reception, Miss Meredith?" he went on, with a smile and a sadder change of tone. "No one to meet me at the depôt, no one to meet me at home! Father and brother at the club, mother and sister amusing themselves in the town."

His remark scarcely seemed to admit of a reply; it was not my place to assure him of his welcome, and I got out of the situation with a smile.

He looked at me again, this time more attentively. "But I fear you were really frightened just now. You are pale still and trembling. Did you think I was a ghost?"

"I thought—I thought you were the Bronzino come down from its frame," I answered, astonished at my own daring. The complete absence of self-consciousness in my companion, the delight, moreover, of being addressed in fluent English, gave me courage.

As I spoke, I moved over half-unconsciously to the picture in question. Andrea, smiling gently, followed me, and planting himself before the canvas contemplated it with a genuine naïve interest that was irresistible.

I stood by, uncertain whether to go or stay, furtively regarding him.

"Was there ever such a creature," I thought; "with your handsome serious face, your gentle dignified air for all the world like Romeo's; with your sweet Italian voice and your ridiculous American accent—and the general suggestion about you of an old bottle with new wine poured in—only in this case by no means to the detriment of the bottle?"

At this point the unconscious object of my meditation broke in upon it.

"Why, yes," said Andrea, calmly, "I had never noticed it before, but I really am uncommonly like the fellow."

As he spoke, he fixed his eyes, frank as a child's, upon my face.

As for me, I could not forbear smiling; whereupon Andrea, struck with the humour of the thing, broke into a radiant and responsive smile. I thought I had never seen any one so funny or so charming.

At this point a bell rang through the house. "That must be my mother," he said, growing suddenly alert. "Miss Meredith, you will excuse me."

I lingered in the gallery after he had left, but my forlorn and pensive mood of ten minutes ago had vanished.

Rather wistfully, but with a certain excitement, I listened to the confused sound of voices which echoed up from below.

Then I heard the whole party pass upstairs behind me, the heels of the ladies clattering in a somewhat frenzied manner on the stones.

Annunziata was laughing and crying, the Marchesa was talking earnestly, the young ladies scattered exclamations as they went. Every now and then I caught the clear tones of Andrea's voice.

At dinner that night there was high festival. Everyone talked incessantly, even Romeo and his father. We had a turkey stuffed with chestnuts, and the Marchese brought forth his choicest wines. At the beginning of the meal I had been introduced to the new arrival, and, for no earthly reason, neither had made mention of the less formal fashion in which we had become acquainted. Some friends dropped in after dinner, and Andrea was again the hero of the hour—a rather trying position, which he bore with astonishing grace. As for me, I sat sewing in a distant corner of the room, content with my spectator's place, growing more and more interested in the spectacle.

"That Costanza!" I thought, rather crossly, as I observed the handsome Contessima smiling archly at Andrea above her fan. "I wonder how long the little comedy will be a-playing? As for the end, that, I suppose, is a foregone conclusion." Then I bent my head over my crewelwork again. I was beginning to feel annoyed with Andrea for having passed over our first meeting in silence; I was beginning also to wish I had furred slippers like Bianca's, as a protection against the cold floor.

"Miss Meredith," said a voice at my elbow, "you are cold; your teeth will soon begin to chatter in your head."

Then, before I knew what was happening, I was led from my corner, and installed close to the kindling logs. And it was Andrea, the hero of the day, who had done this thing; but had done it so quietly, so much as a matter of course, as scarcely to attract attention, though the Marchesa's eye fell on me coldly as I took up my new position.

"It really does make the place more alive," I reflected, as I laid my head on my pillow that night. "I am quite glad the Marchesino is here. And I wonder what he thinks of Costanza?"

VIII

An Italian Ball

The next day was exquisitely bright and warm—we seemed to have leapt at a bound into the very heart of spring—and when I came out of my room I was greeted with the news that Andrea and the ladies had gone to drive in the Cascine. Annunziata was my informant. She had stayed at home, and, freed from the rigid eye of her mother-in-law, was sitting very much at her ease, ready to gossip with the first comer.

The Marchesina could rise to an occasion as well as any one else; could, when duty called, confine her stout form in the stiffest of stays, and build up her hair into the neatest of bandolined pyramids. But I think she was never so happy as when, the bow unbent, she could expand into a loose morning-jacket and twist up her hair into a vague, unbecoming knot behind.

"Dear little signorina," she cried, beckoning me to a seat with her embroidery scissors, "have you heard the good news? Andrea returns no more to America."

"He has arranged matters with Costanza pretty quickly," was my reflection; and at the thought of that easy capitulation, he fell distinctly in my esteem.

"He has accepted a post in England," went on Annunziata. "We shall see him every year, if not oftener. Everyone is overjoyed. It is a step in the right direction. Who knows but one day he may settle in Italy?" And she smiled meaningly, nodding her head as she spoke.

The ladies came back at lunch-time without their cavalier, who had stayed to *collazione* with some relatives in the town.

The afternoon was spent upstairs talking over the dance which was to take place that evening, discussing every detail of costume and every expected guest. Costanza was as cross as two sticks, and hadn't a good word for anybody. We dined an hour earlier than usual, but none of the gentlemen put in an appearance at the meal. With a sigh of inexpressible relief I rose from the table, and escaped to the welcome shelter of my room.

"I thought I was glad that Andrea had come," was my reflection; "but today has been worse than any other day."

Then, rather discontentedly, I began the preparations for my toilet.

The little black net dress, with the half-low bodice, the tan gloves, the black satin shoes, were already lying on the bed.

It is all very well to be Cinderella, if you happen to have a fairy-godmother. Without this convenient relative the situation is far less pleasant, and so common as to be not even picturesque. There are lots of Cinderellas who never went to the ball, or, if they did go, were taken no notice of by the prince, and were completely cut out by the proud sisters. Musing thus, with a pessimism which, to do me justice, was new to me, I proceeded to make myself as fine as the circumstances of the case permitted.

"At least my hair is nice," I thought, as I stood before the glass and fastened a knot of daffodils into my bodice; "Jenny always admired it, and the shape of my head as well. I've been pale and ugly, too, for the last few weeks, but my cheeks are red enough tonight. They are only red from crossness, and the same cause has made my eyes so bright, but how is any one to know that?"

"Why, Elsie Meredith," said a voice suddenly from some inner region of my being, "what on earth is the matter with you? You, who could never be persuaded to take enough interest in your personal appearance! Surely you have caught the infection from that middle-aged Costanza."

With which rather spiteful reflection I blew out the candles, threw a shawl over my shoulders, and ran downstairs into the ball-room.

I was the first arrival. The room stood empty, and I halted a moment on the threshold, struck by the beauty of the scene.

The walls of the vast chamber were hung from top to bottom with faded tapestry, of good design and soft dim colour. From the painted, vaulted ceiling, which rose to mysterious height, hung a chandelier in antique silver, ablaze with innumerable wax lights. Other lights in silver sconces were placed at intervals along the walls, and narrow sofas in faded gilt and damask bordered the wide space of the floor.

At one end of the room was a musician's gallery, whence sounds of tuning were already to be heard.

Two other rooms led out from the main apartment, both of smaller size, indeed, but large withal, and characterized by the same severe beauty. There was no attempt at decoration, nor was any needed.

Having made a general survey of the premises, I advanced to the middle of the ball-room, and began to feel the floor, across which a faded drugget had been stretched, critically with my foot.

Then I circled round on the tips of my toes under the chandelier, humming the air of "Dream Faces" very softly to myself.

So absorbed was I in this occupation that I did not notice the entrance of another person, till suddenly a voice sounded quite close to my ear, "Well, is it a good floor?"

I stopped, blushing deeply. There before me stood Andrea, looking very nice in his evening clothes.

"Not very good, but quite fair," I answered, recovering my self-possession before his complete coolness.

He smiled quietly.

"I guess you are a person of experience in such matters, Miss Meredith."

"I haven't been to many balls, but we are fond of dancing at home."

"We?" said Andrea, interrogatively.

"My sisters—"

"And brothers?"

"I haven't any brothers."

"And friends?"

"Yes, and friends." I could not help laughing; then thinking that he looked rather offended, I added by way of general conversation—

"How beautiful this room looks. It seems quite desecration to dance in it."

He looked round, and up and down.

"Yes, I suppose it is elegant. I think it very gloomy."

Again I found myself smiling. There was something so absurd in this mixture of the soft, sweet Italian tones and the very pronounced American accent, not to speak of the occasional flowers of American idiom.

This time, however, Andrea did not appear offended, but smiled back at me most charmingly, then turned to greet his mother, who, the two girls in her wake, came sweeping across the room in violet velvet and diamonds.

"You are down early, Miss Meredith," she said to me without moving a muscle of her face, but making me feel that I had committed a breach of propriety in venturing alone downstairs.

"You look so nice," cried Bianca, who, in blue-striped silk and a high tortoiseshell comb, had made the very worst of herself.

Costanza, shrugging her shoulders, turned and rustled across the room.

I was surprised to see how handsome she looked. With her gown of richest brocade, made with a long train and Elizabethan collar, with the rubies gleaming in her dark hair and in the folds of her bodice, she seemed a figure well in harmony with the stately beauty of her surroundings. As though conscious of her effect, she moved over to the entrance of the inner room, and stood there framed in the arched doorway with its hangings of faded damask. Andrea went at once to her side.

"It's a long time since we have had a dance together, Contessima."

"A long, long time, Marchesino."

Then their voices fell, and there was nothing to be heard but a twittering exchange of whispers.

Bianca put her arm about my waist and whirled me round and round.

"We don't dance the same way," she said, releasing me after a brief but breathless interval.

Annunziata in apple-green brocade and a pearl stomacher was the next arrival, laughing heartily, and flourishing her lace handkerchief as she came. Behind her strolled her husband, handsome, indolent, and grave as a judge. The old Marchese brought up the rear.

The guests began now to arrive; smart, dignified, voluble matrons; smart, expectant girls; slight, serious young civilians, dandling their hats as they came; pretty little officers in uniform, with an air of being very much at home in a ball-room. Romeo brought me a programme, and wrote his name down for the lancers.

Then I stood there rather forlornly while the musicians struck up the first waltz.

At the first notes of the music Andrea left Costanza's side and came towards me.

"He is going to ask me to dance," was my involuntary reflection; "how nice! I am sure he dances well."

"Let me introduce il signor capitano," said Romeo's voice in my ear; and there stood a trim little person in uniform before me, bowing and requesting the honour of the first dance.

"One moment," said Andrea, quietly, as, rather disappointed, I began to move away with my partner; "Miss Meredith, may I see your card?"

I handed him the little bit of gilt pasteboard, virgin, save for his brother's name.

"Will you give me six and ten?"

"Yes."

He returned to Costanza, his partner for the dance, and I and my officer plunged into the throng.

It was not a success. There were no points of agreement in our practice of waltzing, and after a few turns we subsided on to one of the damask sofas, exchanging commonplaces and watching the dancers, whose rapid twists and bounding action filled my heart with despair.

"I shall never be able to dance like that," I reflected. It was by no means an ungraceful performance. They leapt high, it is true, but in no vulgar fashion of mere jumping; rather they rose into the air with something of the ease and elasticity of an indiarubber ball, maintaining throughout an appearance of great seriousness and dignity.

At the end of the dance, my partner bowed himself away, and I withdrew rather forlornly to a corner, hoping to escape unnoticed. Here, however, Romeo again espied me, and led up to me a rather despondent young gentleman—a student at the University of Pisa, I afterwards learned—whom I had observed nursing his tall silk hat in solitude throughout the previous dance.

I explained earnestly that I could not dance Italian fashion; that I preferred, indeed, to be a spectator, and settled down into my corner with some philosophy.

"I dare say Andrea can waltz my way," I thought, looking down at my programme, where the initials A.B. stood out clearly on two of the gilt lines. "It is rather disappointing to have to sit still and look on while other people dance to this delightful music, but it is amusing enough, in its way, and I must keep my eyes open and remember things to tell the girls."

It annoyed me, I confess, a little to meet Costanza's glance of contemptuous pity as she whirled by with a tall officer, and a mean-spirited desire came over me to explain to her that I was sitting out from choice, and not from necessity. The flood of dancers rushed on—those many-coloured ephemera, on which the old, dim walls looked down so gravely—and still I sat there patiently enough, though my eyes were beginning to ache and my brain to whirl.

Annunziata's apple-green skirts, Bianca's blue and white stripes, the Contessima's brocade and rubies, were growing familiar to weariness, so often did they flash before my sight. It was with genuine relief that I welcomed Romeo, who came up to claim the fifth dance, the lancers, for which he had engaged me at the beginning of the evening.

But alas! the word "lancers" printed in French on the programme proved a mere will-o'-the-wisp, and I found myself drawn into the intricacies of a quite unknown and elaborate dance.

Romeo, gravely piloting me through the confusing maze, was all courtesy and patience; but Andrea, who with Costanza was our *vis-à-vis*, seemed entirely absorbed in observing my stupidity.

"And I am really getting through with it very well," was my reflection; "it is all that Costanza who makes him notice the mistakes."

The next dance was Andrea's—a waltz.

"Have you been having a good time, Miss Meredith?" he asked, as we stood awaiting the music. "I lost sight of you till the lancers, just now."

"I have been sitting in a corner, looking on," I answered dismally, but with a smile.

"What!" he drew his brows together.

"It is no one's fault but my own. I can't waltz Italian fashion. Perhaps we had better not attempt it."

For answer Andrea put his arm scientifically round my waist, piloting me into the middle of the room, where a few couples were already revolving.

"I have yet to find the young lady with whom I could not waltz," he observed, quietly, as we glided smoothly and rapidly across the floor.

Oh, the delights of that waltz! It was one of the intensely good things of life which cannot happen often even in the happiest careers; one of the little bits of perfection which start up now and then to astonish us, plants of such delicate growth that only by an unforeseen succession of accidents are they ever brought to birth. With what ease my partner skimmed about that crowded hall! How skilfully he steered among the bounding complex! Was ever such music heard out of heaven; and was ever such a kind, comfortable, reassuring presence as that of Andrea?

A moment ago I had been bored, wistful, tired; now I had nothing left to wish for.

"Well," he said, as, the music coming to an end, we paused for the first time; "that was not so bad for an Italian, was it?"

I was so happy that I could only smile, and my partner, apparently not disconcerted by my stupidity, led me into the inner room, installed me in a chair, and seated himself in another opposite.

At the same moment Romeo came sauntering up to us, throwing a remark in rapid Italian to his brother.

The latter, with a slight frown, rose reluctantly, and the two men went over to the doorway, where they stood talking.

I fell to observing them with considerable interest, these handsome, dark-eyed gentlemen, with their grace and air of breeding, who were at the same time so curiously alike and so curiously different.

In both the same simplicity and ease was felt to cover a certain inscrutability, the frankness a considerable depth of reserve; and in neither was seen a person to be thwarted with impunity. But whereas in Romeo's case the quiet manner was the unmistakable mark of a genuine indolence and indifference, in Andrea's it only served to bring out more clearly the keen vitality, the alertness, the purpose with which his whole personality was instinct.

I had not much time for my observations. In the course of a few minutes Annunziata rustled smilingly past them, and threw herself and her green skirts into the chair just vacated by her brother-in-law.

The latter shot a quick glance at her, shrugged his shoulders slightly, resumed his conversation with Romeo, and made no attempt to rejoin me.

As for me, my little cup of pleasure was dashed to the ground.

Annunziata, fanning herself and talking volubly, made but a poor substitute for Andrea, and I began to be dimly aware of a certain hostility towards myself in the atmosphere.

The next dance was played, and the next, and still Annunziata sat there smiling. The two gentlemen had long disappeared into the ball-room, and we had the smaller apartment to ourselves.

"I can't stand it any longer," I thought, "even with another waltz with Andrea in prospect." And making an apology to the Marchesina, I stole through a side door upstairs to bed.

Sounds of revelry reached me faint through the thick walls for many succeeding hours; and I lay awake on my great bed till the dawn crept in through the shutters.

"I have been a wallflower," I reflected, "a wallflower, to do me justice, for the first time in my life. And I'm not so sure that, in some respects, it wasn't the nicest dance I ever was at."

IX

"What has Happened to Me?"

"Costanza is so cross," said Bianca, drawing me aside, in her childish fashion; "she talks of going back at once to Florence, and I don't know who would be sorry if she did."

"Oh, for shame, Bianca; she is your guest," I said, really shocked.

It was the morning after the ball, and all the ladies were assembled in the sitting-room, displaying everyone of them unmistakable signs of what is sometimes called "hot coppers."

I had been greeted coldly on my entrance, a fact which had dashed my own cheerful mood, and had set me seriously considering plans of departure. "If they are going to dislike me, there's an end of the matter," I thought; but I hated the idea of retiring beaten from the field.

I did not succeed in making my escape for a single hour throughout the day. Everyone wanted Miss Meredith's services; now she must hold a skein of wool, now accompany Costanza's song on the piano, now shout her uncertain Italian down the trumpet of a deaf old visitor. I was quite worn out by dinner-time; and afterwards the whole party drove off to a reception, leaving me behind.

"Does not the signorina accompany us?" said Andrea to his mother, as they stood awaiting the carriage.

"Miss Meredith is tired and goes to bed," answered the Marchesa in her dry, impenetrable way. I had not been invited, but I made no remark. Andrea opened his eyes wide, and came over deliberately to the sofa where I sat.

There was such a determined look about the lines of his mouth, about his whole presence, that I found myself unconsciously thinking: "You are a very, very obstinate person, Marchesino, and I for one should be sorry to defy you. You looked just like that five years ago, when they were trying to tie you to the ancestral apron-strings, and I don't know that Costanza is to be envied, when all is said."

"Miss Meredith," said his lowered voice in my ear, "this is the first opportunity you have given me today of telling you what I think of your conduct. I do not wonder that you are afraid of me."

"Marchesino!"

"To make engagements and to break them is not thought good behaviour either in Italy or in America. Perhaps in England it is different."

I looked up, and meeting his eyes forgot everything else in the world. Forgot the Marchesa hovering near, only prevented by a certain awe of her son from swooping down on us; forgot Costanza champing the bit, as it were, in the doorway; forgot the cold, unfriendly glances which had made life dark for me throughout the day.

"I had no partner for number ten," went on Andrea, "though a lady had promised to dance it with me. Now what do you think of that lady's behaviour?"

His gravity was too much for my own, and I smiled.

"You suffer from too keen a sense of humour, Miss Meredith," he said, and I scarcely knew whether to take him seriously or not. I only knew that my heart was beating, that my pulses were throbbing as they had never done before.

"The carriage is at the door, Andrea," cried Bianca, bouncing up to us, and looking inquisitive and excited.

He rose at once, holding out his hand.

"Good-night, Miss Meredith," he said, aloud; "I am sorry that you do not accompany us."

Costanza flounced across the passage noisily; the Marchesa looked me full in the face, then turned away in silence; and even Annunziata was grave. I felt suddenly that I had been brought up before a court of justice, tried, and found guilty of some heinous but unknown offence.

Light still lingered in the gallery, and when the carriage had rolled off I sought shelter there, pacing to and fro with rapid, unequal tread. What had happened to me? What curious change had wrought itself not only in myself, but in my surroundings, during these last two days? Was it only two days since Andrea had come towards me down this very gallery? Unconsciously the thought shaped itself, and then I grew crimson in the solitude. What had Andrea to do with the altered state of things? How could his home-coming affect the little governess, the humblest member of that stately household?

There in the glow of the fading sunlight hung the Bronzino, its eyes—so like some other eyes—gazing steadily at me from the canvas. "Beautiful eyes," I thought; "honest eyes, good eyes! There was never anything very bad in that person's life. I think he was good and happy, and that everyone was fond of him."

And then again I blushed, and turned away suddenly. To blush at a picture!

Down in the deserted garden the spring was carrying on her work, in her own rapid, noiseless fashion. No doubt it was the spring also that was stirring in my heart; that was causing all sorts of new, unexpected growths of thought and feeling to sprout into sudden life; that was changing the habitual serenity of my mood into something of the fitfulness of an April day.

Alternately happy and miserable, I continued to pace the gallery till the last remnant of sunlight had died away, and the brilliant moonlight came streaming in through the windows.

Then my courage faded all at once. The stony place struck chill, my own footsteps echoed unnaturally loud; the eyes of the Bronzino staring through the silver radiance, filled me with unspeakable terror.

With a beating heart I gathered up my skirts and fled up the silent stairs, along the corridor, to my room.

X

"As Good as Gold"

Leaning out from the window of my room the next morning, I saw Andrea and his father walking slowly along the Lung' Arno in the sunlight.

In the filial relation, Andrea, I had before observed, particularly shone. His charming manner was never so charming as when he was addressing his father; and the presence of his younger son appeared to have a vitalizing, rejuvenating effect on the old Marchese.

And now, as I watched them pacing amicably in the delightful spring morning, the tears rose for a moment to my eyes; I remembered that it was Sunday, that a long way off in unromantic Islington my mother was making ready for the walk to church, while I, an exile, looked from my palace window with nothing better in prospect than a solitary journey to the *Chiesa Inglese*. Annunziata had not gone to mass, and when I came downstairs ready dressed she explained that she had a headache, and was in need of a little company to cheer her up.

Of course I could not do less than offer to forego my walk and attendance at church, which I did with a wistful recollection of the beauty and sweetness of the day.

"Have you heard?" she said. "Costanza goes back to Florence tonight. She prefers not to miss the last two days of Carnival, Monday and Tuesday. So she says," cried the Marchesina, with a frankness that astonished me, even from her; "so she says; but between ourselves, Andrea was very attentive last night to Emilia di Rossa. Costanza ought to understand what he is by now. She has known him all her life; she ought certainly to be aware that his one little weakness—Andrea is as good as gold—is the ladies."

I bent my head low over my work, with an indignant, shame-stricken consciousness that I was blushing. "He is evidently engaged to Costanza," I thought, and I wished the earth would open and swallow me.

"And a young girl, like Emilia," went on Annunziata; "who knows what construction she might put upon his behaviour? It is not that he says so much, but he has a way with him which is open to misinterpretation. Poor little thing, she has no money to speak of, and, even if she had, who are the Di Rossas? Andrea, for all he is so free and easy, is as proud as the devil, and the very last man to make a *mésalliance*. A convent, say I, will be the end of the Di Rossa." And she sighed contentedly.

Was it possible that she was insulting me? Was this a warning, a warning to me, Elsie Meredith? Did she think me an adventuress, setting traps for a rich and noble husband, or merely an eager fool liable to put a misconstruction on the simplest acts of kindliness and courtesy?

My blazing cheeks, no doubt, confirmed whichever suspicion she had been indulging in, but I was determined to show her that I was not afraid. Lifting my face—with its hateful crimson—boldly to hers, I said: "We in England regard marriage and—and love in another way. I know it is not so in Italy; but with us the reason for getting married is that you are fond of someone, and that someone is fond of you. Other sorts of marriages are not thought nice," with which bold and sweeping statement on behalf of my native land I returned with trembling fingers to my needlework.

To do me justice, I fully believed in my own words. That marriage which had not affection for its basis was shameful had been the simple creed of the little world at home.

"Indeed?" said Annunziata, with genuine interest; "but, as you say, it is not so with us."

My lips twitched in an irresistible smile. Her round eyes met mine so frankly, her round face was so unruffled in its amiability, that I could not but feel I had made a fool of myself. The guileless lady was prattling on, no doubt as usual, as a relief to her own feelings, and not with any underlying intention.

I felt more ashamed than before of my own self-consciousness.

"What is the matter with you, Elsie Meredith?" cried a voice within me. "I think your own mother wouldn't know you; your own sisters would pass you by in the street."

"Andrea ought to know," went on Annunziata, "that such freedom of manners is not permissible in Italy between a young man and young women. He seems to have forgotten this in America, where, I am told, the licence is something shocking."

I wished the good lady would be less confidential—what was all this to me?—and I was almost glad when the ladies came sailing in from mass, all of them evidently in the worst possible tempers.

There was an air of constraint about the whole party at lunch that day. Wedged in between the Marchesa and Romeo I sat silent and glum, having returned Andrea's cordial bow very coldly across the table. Everyone deplored Costanza's approaching departure, rather mechanically, I thought, and that young lady herself repeatedly expressed her regret at leaving.

"Dear Marchesa," she cried, "I am at my wits' end with disappointment; but my mother's letter this morning admits of but one reply. She says she cannot spare me from the gaieties of the next two days."

"You might come back after Ash Wednesday," said Bianca, who sat with her arm round her friend between the courses, and whose friendship seemed to have been kindled into a blaze by the coming separation.

"Dearest Bianca, if I could only persuade you to return with me!"

"Bianca never makes visits," answered her mother, drily.

"Were you at church this morning, Miss Meredith?" asked the old Marchese, kindly, as the figs and chestnuts were put on the table.

It was the first time that any one had addressed me directly throughout the meal, and I blushed hotly as I gave my answer.

The departure of Costanza, her boxes and her maid, was of course the great event of the afternoon.

The three gentlemen and Annunziata drove with her to the station, and I was left behind with my pupil and her mother.

A stiff bow from Costanza, a glare through her double eyeglass, and a contemptuous "Good-bye, Miss," in English, had not tended to raise my spirits. To be an object of universal dislike was an experience as new as it was unpleasant, and I was losing confidence in myself with every hour.

Even Bianca had deserted me, and, ensconced close to her mother, shot glances at me of her early curiosity and criticism.

As for the Marchesa, that inscrutable person scarcely stopped talking all the afternoon, rattling on in her dry, colourless way about nothing at all. Speech was to her the shield and buckler which silence is to persons less gifted. Behind her own volubility she could withdraw as behind a bulwark, whence she made observations safe from being herself observed.

I was quite worn out by eight o'clock, when the usual Sunday visitors began to arrive.

With my work in my hand, I sat on the outskirts of the throng, not working indeed, but pondering deeply.

"Miss Meredith, you are very industrious."

There before me stood Andrea, a very obstinate look on his face, unmindful of Annunziata's proximity and Romeo's scowls.

"As it happens, I haven't put in a stitch for the last ten minutes," I answered quietly, though my heart beat.

He drew a chair close to mine.

"You are unfair, Andrea, you are unfair," I thought, "to make things worse for Miss Meredith by singling her out in this way, when you know it makes them all so cross. Things are bad enough for her as it is, and you might forego your little bit of amusement."

I began really to stitch with unnatural industry, bending an unresponsive face over the work in my hand.

"That is very pretty," said Andrea.

"No, no, Marchesino," I thought again, "you are as good as gold, any one could see that from your eyes; but you have a little weakness, only one—'the ladies'—and you must not be encouraged."

I turned to Annunziata, who, baffled by the English speech, sat perplexed and helpless.

"Marchesina," I said aloud in Italian, "the Marchesino admires my work."

"I taught her how to do it," cried Annunziata, breaking into a smile. "See, it is not so easy to draw the fine gold thread through the leather, but she is an apt pupil."

"Miss Meredith, I am sorry to see you looking so pale." Andrea dropped his voice very low, adhering obstinately to English and fixing his eyes on mine.

"I haven't been out today."

"What, wasting this glorious weather indoors. Is it possible that you are falling into the worst of our Italian ways?"

"I generally go for a walk."

I rose as I spoke, and turned to the Marchesina. "I am so tired; do you think I may be excused?"

"Certainly, dear child."

Bowing to the assembled company I made my way deliberately to the door. Andrea was there before me, holding it open, a look of unusual sternness on his face.

"Good-night, Miss Meredith," and then before them all he held out his hand.

Only for a moment did our fingers join in a firm eager clasp, only for a moment did his eyes meet mine in a strange, mysterious glance. Only for a moment, but as I fled softly, rapidly along the corridor I felt that in that one instant of time all my life's meaning had been changed. "As good as gold; as good as gold." These words went round and round in my head as I lay sobbing on the pillow.

Somehow that was the only part of Annunziata's warning which remained with me.

XI

"Will You Make Me Very Happy?"

I rose early next morning, and without waiting for my breakfast, ran downstairs, made Pasquale, the vague servant, open the door for me, and I escaped into the sunshine.

In the long and troubled night just passed I had come to a resolution—I would go home.

From first to last, I told myself, the experiment had been a failure. From first to last I had been out of touch with the people with whom I had come to dwell; the almost undisguised hostility of the last few days was merely the culmination of a growing feeling.

In that atmosphere of suspicion, of disapprobation, I could exist no longer. Defeated, indeed, but in no wise disgraced, I would return whence I came. I would tell them everything at home, and they would understand.

That I had committed some mysterious breach of Italian etiquette, outraged some notion of Italian propriety, I could not doubt; but at least I had been guilty of nothing of which, judged by my own standard, I could feel ashamed.

But my heart was very heavy as I sped on through the streets, instinctively making my way to the cathedral.

It was the second week in March, and the spring was full upon us. The grass in the piazza smelt of clover, and here and there on the brown hills was the flush of blossoming peach or the snow of flowering almonds.

In the soft light of the morning, cathedral, tower, and baptistery seemed steeped in a divine calm. Their beauty filled me with a great sadness. They were my friends; I had grown to love them, and now I was leaving them, perhaps for ever.

Pacing up and down, and round about, I tried to fix my thoughts on my plans, to consider with calmness my course of action. But this was the upshot of all my endeavours, the one ridiculous irrelevant conclusion at which I could arrive—"He is certainly not engaged to Costanza."

As I came round by the main door of the cathedral for perhaps the twentieth time, I saw Andrea walking across the grass towards me.

A week ago, I had never seen his face; now as I watched him advancing in the sunlight, it seemed that I had known him all my life. Never was figure more familiar, never presence more reassuring, than that of this stranger. The sight of him neither disturbed nor astonished me; now that he was here, his coming seemed inevitable, part of the natural order of things.

"Ah, I have found you," he said quietly, and we turned together and strolled towards the Campo Santo.

"Do you often come here?" He stopped and looked at me dreamily.

"Often, often. It is all so beautiful and so sad."

"It is very sad."

"Do you not see how very beautiful it is?" I cried, "that there is nothing like it in the whole world? And I am leaving it, and it breaks my heart!"

"You are going away?"

"Yes." I was calm no longer, but strangely agitated. I turned away, and began pacing to and fro.

"Ah! they have not made you happy?" His eyes flashed as he came up to me.

"No," I said, "I am not happy; but it is nobody's fault. They do not like me, and I cannot bear it any more. It has never happened to me before—no one has thought me very wonderful, very clever, very beautiful, very brilliant; but people have always liked me, and if I am not liked I shall die."

With which foolish outbreak—which astonished no one more than the speaker—I turned away again with streaming eyes.

"Let us come in here," said Andrea, still with that strange calm in voice and manner, and together we passed into the Campo Santo.

A bird was singing somewhere among the cypresses; the daffodils rose golden in the grass; the strip of sky between the cloisters was intensely blue.

"Miss Meredith," said Andrea, taking my hand, "will you make me very happy—will you be my wife?"

We were standing in the grass-plot, face to face, and he was very pale.

His words seemed the most natural thing in the world. I ought, perhaps, to have made a protest, to have reminded him of family claims and dues, to have made sure that love, not chivalry, was speaking.

But I only said, "Yes," very low, looking at him as we stood there among the tombs, under the blue heavens.

AMY LEVY

"As you came down the gallery, in the sunlight, with the little grey gown, and the frightened look in the modest eyes, I said to myself, 'Here, with the help of God, comes my wife!'"

I do not know how long we had been in the cloisters, pacing slowly, hand in hand, almost in silence. The sun was high in the heavens, and the bird in the cypresses sang no more.

"Do you know," cried Andrea, stopping suddenly, and laughing, "here is a most ridiculous thing! What is your name? for I haven't the ghost of an idea!"

"Elsie." I laughed, too. The joke struck us both as an excellent one.

"Elsie! Ah, the sweet name! Elsie, Elsie! Was ever such a dear little name? What shall we do next, Elsie, my friend?"

"Take me to the mountains!" I cried, suddenly aware that I was tired to exhaustion, that I had had no sleep and no breakfast. "Take me to the mountains; I have longed, longed for them all these days!"

I staggered a little, and closed my eyes.

When I opened them he was holding me in his arms, looking down anxiously at my face.

"Yes, we will go to the mountains; but first I shall take you home, and give you something to eat and drink, Elsie."

XII

The Breaking of the Storm

Y ou are not afraid?" said Andrea, as we turned on to the Lung' Arno and came in sight of the house.

"No," I answered in all good faith, a little resenting the question.

After all, what was there to fear? This was the nineteenth century, when people's marriages were looked upon as their own affairs, and the paternal blessing—since it had ceased to be a *sine quâ non*—was never long withheld.

If Andrea's family were disappointed in his choice, and I supposed that at first such would be the case, it lay with me to turn that disappointment into satisfaction.

I had but a modest opinion of myself, yet I knew that in making me his wife Andrea was doing nothing to disgrace himself; his good taste, perhaps, was at fault, but that was all.

You see, I had been educated in a very primitive and unworldly school of manners, and must ask you to forgive my ignorance.

Yet I confess my heart did beat rather fast as we made our way up the steps into the empty hall, and I wished the next few hours well over.

I reminded myself that I was under Andrea's wing, safe from harm, but looking up at Andrea I was not quite sure of his own unruffled self-possession. A distant hum of voices greeted us as we entered, growing louder with every stair we mounted, and when we reached the landing leading to the gallery, there stood the whole family assembled like the people in a comedy.

To judge from the sounds we heard, they had been engaged in excited discussion, everyone speaking at once, but at our appearance a dead and awful silence fell upon the group.

Slowly we advanced, the mark of every eye, then came to a stop well in front of the group.

It seemed an age, but I believe it was less than a minute, before the Marchesa stepped forward, looking straight at me and away from her son, so as not in the least to include him in her condemnation, and said: "I am truly sorry, Miss Meredith, for I was given to understand that your mother was a very respectable woman."

"Mother!" cried Andrea, with a pale face and flashing eyes; "be careful of your words." Then taking my hand, he turned to the old Marchese, who stood helpless and speechless in the background, and said loudly and deliberately: "This lady has promised to be my wife."

For an instant no one spoke, but there was no mistaking the meaning of their silence; then Romeo called out in a voice of suppressed fury: "It is impossible!"

Andrea, still holding my hand, turned with awful calm upon his brother. Annunziata's ready tears were flowing, and Bianca gazed open-mouthed with horror and excitement upon the scene.

"Romeo," said Andrea, tightening his hold of my fingers, "this is no affair of yours. Once before you tried to interfere in my life; I should have thought the result had been too discouraging for a second attempt."

"It is the affair of all of us when you try to bring disgrace on the family."

"Disgrace! Sir, do you know what word you are using, and in reference to whom?"

"Oh, the signorina, of course, is charming. I have nothing to say against her."

He bowed low, and, as our eyes met, I knew he was my enemy.

"Andrea," said his mother, interposing between her sons, "this is no time and place for discussion. Miss Meredith shall come with me, and you shall endeavour to explain to your father how it is you have insulted him."

"My son," said the Marchese, speaking for the first time, with a certain mournful dignity, "never before has such a thing happened in our family as that a wife should be brought home to it without the head of the house being consulted. What am I to think of this want of confidence, of respect, except that you are ashamed of your choice?"

"Father," answered Andrea, drawing my hand through his arm, "it has throughout been my intention of asking your consent and your blessing. Nor has there been any concealment on my part. From the first I have expressed my admiration of this lady very openly to you all. What is the result? that she is watched, persecuted like a suspected criminal, and finally driven away—she a young girl, a stranger in a foreign land. Can you expect the man who loves her to stand by and see this without letting her know at the first opportunity that there is one on whose protection she can at once and always rely?"

"Andrea," said his mother, "we did but try our best to prevent what we one and all regard as a misfortune. Miss Meredith is no suitable bride for a son of the house of Brogi. Oh" (as he opened his lips as about to protest), "I have nothing to say against her, though indeed you cannot expect me to be lost in admiration of her discretion."

The Marchesa shrugged her shoulders and threw out her hands as she spoke, with an impatience which she rarely displayed.

Andrea answered very quietly: "My mother, this is no time and place for such a discussion. With your permission, I will retire with my father, and Miss Meredith shall withdraw to her own room." He released my hand very gently from his arm, and stood a moment looking down at me.

"You are not afraid, Elsie?" he whispered in English.

"Yes, I am frightened to death!"

"It will be all right very soon."

"Must you leave me, Andrea?"

"Yes, dear, I must."

He went over to his father and gave him his arm. All this time Annunziata was weeping like the walrus in "Alice," her loud sobs echoing dismally throughout the house.

"Elsie," said Andrea, as he prepared to descend with the Marchese, "go straight to your room."

I turned without a word, and stunned, astonished, unutterably miserable, fled upstairs without a glance at the hostile group on the landing.

Once the door safely shut behind me, my pent up feelings found vent, and I sobbed hysterically.

Was ever such a morning in a woman's life? And I had had no breakfast.

I was not allowed much time in which to indulge my emotions. Very soon came a knock at the door, and a maid entered with wine, bread, and chestnuts. With the volubility of Italian servants, she pressed me to eat and drink, and when she departed with the empty tray I felt refreshed, and ready to fight my battle to the last. A second knock at the door was not long in following the first, and this time it was the Marchesa who responded to my "Come in."

My heart sank considerably as the stately little lady advanced towards me, and I inwardly reproached Andrea for his desertion.

XIII

A Skilful Diplomatist

M iss Meredith," said the Marchesa, taking the chair I mechanically offered her, and waving her hand towards another, "pray be seated."

I obeyed, feeling secretly much in awe of the rigid little figure sitting very upright opposite me.

"What, after all, is the love of a young man but a passing infatuation?"

This was the first gun fired into the enemy's camp, but there was no answering volley.

That she spoke in all good faith I fully believe, and I felt how useless would be any discussion between us of the point. I looked down in silence.

"Miss Meredith," went on the dry, fluent tones, which I was beginning to feel were the tones of doom, "I will refrain from blaming you in this unfortunate matter. I will merely state the case as it stands. You come into this family, are well received, kindly treated, and regarded with esteem by us all. In return for this, I am bound to say, you perform your duties and do what is required of you with amiability. So far all is well. But there are traditions, feelings, sacred customs, and emotions belonging to the family where you have been received of which you can have no knowledge. That is not required, nor expected of you. What is expected of you, as of every right-minded person, is that you should at least respect what is of such importance to others. Is this the case? Have you not rather taken delight in outraging our feelings in their most delicate relations; in trampling, in your selfish ignorance, on all that we hold most dear?"

Her words stung me; they were cruel words, but I had sworn inwardly to stand by my guns.

With hands interlocked and drooping head, I sat before her without word.

"We had looked forward to this home-coming of my son," she went on, branching off into another talk, "as to the beginning of a fresh epoch of our lives, his father and I, we that are no longer young. To him we had looked for the carrying on of our race. From my daughter-in-law we have been obliged to despair of issue. Andrea, suitably married and established in the home of his ancestors, is what we all dreamed one day to see—nor do I even now entirely abandon the hope of seeing it."

With burning cheeks, and an awful sense that a web was being woven about me, I rose stiffly from my seat, and went over to a cabinet where stood my mother's portrait.

I looked a moment at the pictured eyes, as if for guidance, then said in a low voice:

"Marchesa, I have given my word to your son, and only at his bidding can I take it back."

"It does not take much penetration," she replied, "to know that my son is the last person to bid you do anything of the kind. That he is the soul of chivalry, that the very fact of a person being in an unfortunate position would of itself attract his regard, a child might easily discover."

She spoke with such genuine feeling that for a moment my heart went out towards her; for a moment our eyes met, and not unkindly.

"No doubt," she went on, after a pause, and rising from her seat, "no doubt you represented the precautions we thought necessary to adopt, for your own protection as well my son's, as a form of persecution. If you did not actually represent it to him, I feel sure you gave him to understand that such was the case."

She had hit the mark.

With an agonizing rush of shame, of despair, I remembered my own outbreak on the piazza that morning; how I had confided to Andrea, unasked, my intention of going away, and of the sorrow the prospect gave me.

Had I been mistaken? Had the message of his eyes, his voice, his manner, meant nothing? Had I indeed been unmindful of my woman's modesty? The Marchesa was aware at once of having struck home, and the monotonous tones began again.

"Of course, Miss Meredith, if you choose to take advantage of my son's chivalry, and of his passing fancy—for Andrea is exceedingly susceptible and, no doubt, believes himself in love with you—if, I say, you choose to do this, there is no more to be said.

"Andrea will never take back his word, on that you may rely. But be sure of this, his life will be spoiled, and he will know it. It is not to be expected that you should realize the meaning of ancestral pride, of family honour. Perhaps you think the sentiments which have taken centuries to grow can wither up in a day before the flame of a foolish fancy?"

She had conquered. Moving over to her I looked straight in her face. My voice rang strange and hollow: "By marrying your son I should bring no disgrace upon him nor his family. But I do not intend to marry him."

She had not anticipated so easy a victory. Her cheek flushed, almost as if with compunction. She held out her hands towards me.

But as for me, I turned away ungraciously, and, going up to the chest, began to lift out my under linen, and to pile it on the bed.

"Marchesa, do not thank me, do not praise me? I do not know if I am doing right or wrong."

"Signorina, you have taken the course of an honourable woman."

I went over to the corner where my box stood, and lifted the lid with trembling hands.

"Marchesa, will your servant find out what hour of the night the train leaves for Genoa? and will he have a drosky ready in time to take me to the station?"

"Miss Meredith, there is no necessity for this haste. You cannot depart like this, and without advising your family."

I laid a dress—the little black dress I had worn at the dance—at the bottom of the box. It ought to have gone at the top, but such details did not occupy me at the moment.

"I trust," I said, "that there may be no difficulties placed in the way of my immediate departure."

She came up to me in some agitation.

"But, signorina!"

"Marchesa," I answered, "you have my promise. Is not that what you wanted?"

I intended a dismissal, I frankly own it, but the Marchesa took my rudeness with such humility that for the moment I felt ashamed of myself.

"You have forced me, Miss Meredith, to speak to you as I have never spoken before to a stranger beneath my roof. To fly in the face of the hospitable traditions of the house—"

There came a knock at the door, and the servant announced that the Marchesino desired to speak with Miss Meredith.

We two women, who both loved Andrea, looked at one another.

"You will have to tell him yourself, signorina; from no one else would my son receive your message." The Marchesa turned away as she spoke.

"I will write to him."

Hastily dismissing the servant with words to the effect that Andrea should be waited on in a few minutes, the Marchesa handed me, in silence, the little paper-case which lay on the table. With uncertain fingers I wrote:

MARCHESINO,

We were both of us hasty and ill-advised this morning. I must thank you for the great honour you have done me, but at the same time I must beg of you to release me from the promise I have made.

ELSIE MEREDITH

I handed the open sheet to the Marchesa, who read it carefully, folded it up, thanked me and went from the room.

Then suddenly the great bed began to waltz, the open box in the corner, the painted ceiling, the chest and cabinet to whirl about in hopeless confusion. I don't know how it came about, but for the first time in my life I fainted.

XIV

Released from her Vow

I t was four o'clock in the afternoon; already the front of the house was in shadow, and the drawing-room was cool and dark. Here Andrea and I were standing face to face; both pale, both resolute, while the Marchesa looked from one to the other with anxious eyes.

"You wrote this?" he asked, holding up my unfortunate scrawl.

"Yes, I wrote it."

"And you meant what you wrote?"

"Yes."

He came a little nearer to me, speaking, it seemed, with a certain passionate contempt.

"And you expected me, Elsie, to accept such an answer?"

Before the fire of his glance my eyes fell suddenly. "I have no other answer to give you," I murmured brokenly.

The Marchesa, who had stayed in the room by my own request, glanced questioningly from one to the other, evidently unable to follow the rapid English of the dialogue.

"Is it possible, Elsie, that you have deceived me? That you, who seemed so true, are falser than words can say? Have you forgotten what you said to me, what your eyes said as well as your lips, a few short hours ago?"

"I have not forgotten, but I cannot marry you."

"Then you do not love me, Elsie? you have been amusing yourself."

"If you choose to think so, I cannot help it."

"Elsie, whatever promise you have made to my mother, whatever promise may have been extorted from you, remember that your first promise and your duty were to me."

I shivered from head to foot, while my heart echoed his words. But I had given my word, and I would not go back from it. Never should my mother's daughter thrust herself unwelcomed in any house.

"Have you nothing to say to me, Elsie?"

"Nothing."

"Mother," he cried, turning flashing eyes to the Marchesa, "what have you been saying to her, by what means have you so transformed her, how have you succeeded in wringing from her a most unjust promise?"

"Stay," I interposed, speaking also in Italian, "no promise has been wrung from me, I gave it freely. Marchesino, it seems you cannot believe it, yet it is true that of my own free will I refuse to marry you, that I take back my unconsidered word of this morning. I am no wife for you, and you no husband for me; a few hours of reflection have sufficed very plainly to show me that."

He stood there, paler than ever, looking at me with a piteous air of incredulity. "Elsie, it is not possible—consider, remember—it is not true!"

His voice broke, wavered, and fell; from the passionate entreaty of his eyes I turned my own way.

"It is true, Marchesino, that I will never, never marry you."

Clear, cold, and cruel, though very low, were the tones of my voice; I know not what angel or fiend was giving me strength and utterance; I only know that it was not the normal Elsie who thus spoke and acted.

There was a pause, which seemed to last an age, then once again his voice broke the stillness.

"Since, then, you choose to spoil my life, Elsie, and perhaps (who knows?) your own, there is no more to be said. Far be it from me to extort a woman's consent from her. The only love worth having is that which is given freely, which has courage, which has pride."

Very hard and contemptuous sounded his words. My heart cried out in agony; "Andrea, you are unjust!" but I stood there dumb as a fish, with clasped hands and a drooping head.

"Mother," went on Andrea, "will you kindly summon my father and the others. Miss Meredith, oblige me and stay a few moments; I am sorry to trouble you."

They came in slowly through the open door, the old man, his son and the two younger ladies, anxious, expectant.

Andrea turned towards them.

"My father," he said, "this lady refuses to marry me, and no doubt everybody is content. That she declines to face the hostility, the discourtesy of my family, is not perhaps greatly to be wondered at. It is evident that I am not considered worthy of so great a sacrifice on her part; I do not blame her; rather I blame my own credulity in thinking my love returned. But I wish you all to know," he added, "that I have entirely altered my plans. I shall write off my appointment in England, and shall start tonight for Livorno, on my way to America. My mother, you will kindly send for an *orario* that I may know at what time to order the carriage. Miss Meredith, I bid you good-bye."

He turned round suddenly and faced me, holding out his hand with an air of ceremony.

As for me, I glanced from the dear hand, the dear eyes, to the circle of dismayed faces beyond, then, without a word, I rushed through the open door to my room.

Not daring to allow myself a moment's thought, I fell to immediately packing—fitting in a neat mosaic of stockings and petticoats as though it were the one object of existence.

I do not know if it were minutes or hours before the Marchesa came in, pale and unusually agitated, with no air of enjoying her victory.

"Signorina," she said, "the train for Genoa leaves at 8; I have ordered the carriage for 7.15. You would prefer, perhaps, to dine in your room?"

"I do not wish for dinner, thank you."

"You must allow me to thank you once again, Miss Meredith."

"Do not thank me," I cried, with sudden passion; "I have done nothing to be thanked for."

For, indeed, I was enjoying none of the compensations of martyrdom; for me it was the pang without the palm, as the poet says.

I had fallen in a cause in which I did not believe, had been pressed into a service for which I had no enthusiasm.

"If you will excuse me, Marchesa," I went on, "there are some books of mine in the schoolroom which I must fetch;" and with a little bow, I swept into the corridor with an air as stately as her own.

Andrea's room was on the same floor as my own, but at the other end of the passage, and I had to pass it on my way to the schoolroom. The door stood wide open, and just outside was a large trunk, which Pasquale, the servant, was engaged in packing, while his master gave directions and handed things from the threshold.

I heard their voices as I came.

"At what time does the train go for Livorno, did you say?"

"At 9, *excellenza*. The carriage will be back in time from the station."

I glided past as rapidly as possible, filled with a certain mournful humour at this spectacle of the gentleman packing his box at one end of the hall, while the lady packed hers at the other.

My room was empty when I regained it, and with a heavy heart I finished my sad task, locking the box, labelling and strapping it.

Then I put on my grey travelling dress, my hat, veil, and gloves, and sat down by the window.

It was only half-past five, and these preparations were a little premature; but this confused, chaotic day seemed beyond the ordinary measurements of time.

A maid-servant, with a dainty little dinner on a tray, was the next arrival on the scene. She set it down on a table near me, but I took no heed. As if I could have swallowed a mouthful!

I was quite calm now, only unutterably mournful. "I have spoilt my life," I thought, as my eyes fixed themselves drearily on the river, the old houses opposite, the marble bridge—once all so strange, now grown so dear; "I have spoilt my life, and for what? Ah, if mother had only been here to stand by me! But I was alone. What was I to do? Oh, Andrea, do you hate me?"

The tears streamed down my face as I sat. "Oh, my beloved Pisa," I thought again, "how can I bear to leave you!"

Once more came a knock at the door—the little, quick knock of the Marchesa; and as I responded duly, I reflected: "No doubt she comes to insult me with my salary. And the worst of it is, I shall have to take it; for if I don't, how am I to get home?"

She looked very unlike her usual, self-possessed self as she came towards me.

"Miss Meredith, my husband wishes to speak to you."

I rose wearily in mechanical obedience, and followed her, silent and dejected, downstairs to the Marchese's room. Here, amid his books and papers, sat the old man, looking the picture of wretchedness.

"Ah, signorina," he said, "what will you think of me, of us all? Of the favour which, very humbly, I have to beg of you? I cannot bear thus to part from my son; he is going far away from me, in anger, for an indefinite time. It is you, and you only, who can persuade him to stop!"

I look up in sudden astonishment.

"My child, go to him; tell him that he can stay."

"Marchese, I am sorry, but you ask what is impossible."

"I do not wonder," he said, with a most touching yet dignified humility, "I do not wonder at your reply. My wife, it is your part to speak to this lady."

With set lips yet unblanching front, the gallant little Marchesa advanced.

"Miss Meredith, do not in this matter consider yourself bound by any promise you have made to me. I release you from it."

"May not the matter be considered ended?" I cried in very weariness; "that I have come between your son and his family no one regrets more than I. Only let me go away!"

The old man rose slowly, left the room, and went to the foot of the stairs.

"Andrea, Andrea," I heard him call.

"His excellency has not finished packing," answered the voice of Pasquale.

"Andrea, Andrea," cried his father again; then came rapid footsteps, and in a few seconds Andrea stood once more before me.

He turned from one to the other questioningly.

The Marchese took my hand.

"My son," he said, "can you not persuade this lady to remain with us."

He looked up, my Andrea, and our eyes met; but on neither side was speech or movement.

The old man went on.

"Andrea, it is possible that we did wrong, your mother and I, in attempting to interfere with you in this matter. You must forgive us if we are slow to understand the new spirit of radicalism which, it seems, is the spirit of the times. Once before our wishes clashed; but, my son, I cannot bear to send you away in anger a second time. As for this lady, she knows how deeply we all respect her. Persuade her to forgive us, if indeed you can."

Andrea I saw was deeply moved; he shaded his eyes with his hand, and the tears flowed down my own cheeks unchecked.

"Well, Elsie, it is for you to decide." He spoke at last, coldly, in an off-hand manner.

I was lacking in pride, perhaps in dignity, for though I said nothing, I held out my hand.

"Are you quite sure you love me, Elsie?"

"Quite, quite sure, Andrea."

"I AM SO GLAD," CRIED Bianca, some ten minutes later, giving me a hug, "I am so glad it is you and not that bad-tempered Costanza."

"We are all glad," said the old Marchese, holding out his hand with a smile, while Romeo and his mother stood bearing their defeat with commendable grace.

So it came to pass that on the evening of that wonderful day Andrea and I, instead of being borne by express trains to Genoa and Leghorn respectively, were pacing the gallery arm in arm in the sunlight.

We had been engaged in this occupation for about an hour, and now he knew all about my mother and sisters, and the details of the happy life at Islington.

"We will live in England, but every year we will come to Italy," he was saying, as we paused before the Bronzino, which seemed to have taken in the situation.

"I love Italy more than any place in the world," I answered.

A pause.

"We will be married immediately after Easter, Elsie!"

"Andrea, I go home the day after tomorrow."

"And tomorrow," he said, "we will go to the mountains."

A Note About the Author

Amy Levy (1861–1889) was a British poet and novelist. Born in Clapham, London to a Jewish family, she was the second oldest of seven children. Levy developed a passion for literature in her youth, writing a critique of Elizabeth Barrett Browning's *Aurora Leigh* and publishing her first poem by the age of fourteen. After excelling at Brighton and Hove High School, Levy became the first Jewish student at Newnham College, Cambridge, where she studied for several years without completing her degree. Around this time, she befriended such feminist intellectuals as Clementina Black, Ellen Wordsworth Darwin, Eleanor Marx, and Olive Schreiner. As a so-called "New Woman" and lesbian, much of Levy's literary work explores the concerns of nineteenth century feminism. Levy was a romantic partner of Violet Paget, a British storyteller and scholar of Aestheticism who wrote using the pseudonym Vernon Lee. Her first novel, *The Romance of a Shop* (1888), is powerful story of sisterhood and perseverance in the face of poverty and marginalization. Levy is also known for such poetry collections as *A Minor Poet and Other Verse* (1884) and *A London Plane-Tree and Other Verse* (1889). At the age of 27, after a lifetime of depression exacerbated by relationship trouble and her increasing deafness, Levy committed suicide at her parents' home in Endsleigh Gardens.

A Note from the Publisher

Spanning many genres, from non-fiction essays to literature classics to children's books and lyric poetry, Mint Edition books showcase the master works of our time in a modern new package. The text is freshly typeset, is clean and easy to read, and features a new note about the author in each volume. Many books also include exclusive new introductory material. Every book boasts a striking new cover, which makes it as appropriate for collecting as it is for gift giving. Mint Edition books are only printed when a reader orders them, so natural resources are not wasted. We're proud that our books are never manufactured in excess and exist only in the exact quantity they need to be read and enjoyed.

Discover more of your favorite classics with Bookfinity™.

- Track your reading with custom book lists.
- Get great book recommendations for your personalized Reader Type.
- Add reviews for your favorite books.
- AND MUCH MORE!

Visit **bookfinity.com** and take the fun Reader Type quiz to get started.

Enjoy our classic and modern companion pairings!